"Why did Kit have to go?"

Sean sat beside his daughter and put his arm around her shoulder, fragile as a bird's wing. "Kit's not part of the family, hon."

"Why'd you follow her?"

"I...thought Kit's feelings might be hurt. I wanted to apologize."

"Aunt Mariah wasn't real friendly to her."

"No, she wasn't." He chucked Alex under the chin. "Hey, sport, if you want to see your new cousin, we'd better get a move on."

Alex stayed put. It was no secret she'd inherited his stubborn streak. "I like Kit."

"I know you do." He rubbed the back of his neck, massaged the tense muscles. "And she likes you. There's nothing wrong with that."

What was wrong was his inappropriate attraction to a woman who rocked his sense of responsibility. When she'd jumped on her motorcycle, his first thought had been to climb on with her.

"I just wanna be her friend," Alex whispered. "I don't understand what's going on."

"Kit only came back because her mother messed up and she has to help her out. She's not happy about it and she can't wait to leave. Alex, honey, it's hard to make friends with a person who has no intention of sticking around."

Dear Reader,

When I was in my early twenties and just starting out in the world, I used to play a mind game to help me cope with people who drove me nuts. I would imagine the difficult person and me in a very personal situation far removed from any situation we'd face in reality. My scenario might place me at a table for two with the guy who sold newspapers on the street corner and who could never manage to be civil. I would submerge myself in the fantasy, thinking what could I find out about this person that would make him more human? Perhaps the tough guy rescued stray dogs or ran the volunteer book cart on the hospital pediatrics ward. The fantasy never repaired these individuals' real-time annoying habits; the exercise just reminded me that things—especially other people's lives—are never as they seem. It made me more accepting.

Acceptance is such a simple word, but it appears to be a difficult concept to implement. In *The Trick to Getting a Mom*, Kit Darling has never been accepted in her hometown. She is an outcast and a rebel, surviving only by forging a who-cares exterior and an itinerant lifestyle. Sean McCabe seems to accept his role as a single parent, but beneath the surface simmers a wanderlust that bows before family responsibility. One rootless, the other rooted, the two resist an unacceptable attraction. It takes an eight-year-old, Sean's daughter, Alex, to teach the adults true acceptance.

Amy Frazier

The Trick to
Getting a Mom
Amy Frazier

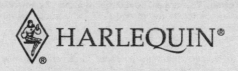

HARLEQUIN®

TORONTO • NEW YORK • LONDON
AMSTERDAM • PARIS • SYDNEY • HAMBURG
STOCKHOLM • ATHENS • TOKYO • MILAN • MADRID
PRAGUE • WARSAW • BUDAPEST • AUCKLAND

ISBN 0-373-71269-3

THE TRICK TO GETTING A MOM

www.eHarlequin.com

Printed in U.S.A.

The Trick to
Getting a Mom

PROLOGUE

WHAT KIND OF FATHER WAS HE if he couldn't keep one little girl out of trouble?

His gut in a knot, Sean McCabe pushed through the double doors of Pritchard's Neck Elementary School. Alex, his eight-year-old daughter, had been suspended from school. For fighting.

At the end of the long echoing corridor that smelled of floor wax and chalk dust, Alex sat outside the principal's office, alone, perched on an enormous bench that made her seem very, very small. Small and adrift on a sea of polished tile.

She looked up, and, even from a distance, Sean could see the shiner, reddish-purple and puffed and already closing one eye.

Instinctively, he rushed to her. "What happened?"

"I finished my work before everybody else," she replied, her head cocked at a defiant angle. "So I raised my hand to go to the bathroom."

"And?" Sean prodded, suspicious. Alex had a way of complicating simple tasks.

"And I thought about how Seafaring Cecil—" Seafaring Cecil was Alex and Sean's favorite travel writer "—says you can adventure anywhere just by drawing a map."

"So…?" Sean didn't trust this train of thought. Alex had inherited his wandering soul, and, more and more in her "explorations," she pushed the limits of what he considered safe for her.

"So I started a map on one of the paper towels from the bathroom with a pencil I found wedged behind a radiator, and I ended up in the fifth-grade-wing."

This wasn't the first time Alex had strayed. Or the first shaggy-dog explanation she'd given Sean. It was, however, the first time his daughter faced suspension from school for her adventuring.

He leveled a stern look at her. "Ms. Simmons told me you were fighting."

With a stubborn one-eyed squint that showed no sign of tears, Alex met and matched his steady gaze. "I hit a fifth grader." She sounded neither proud nor remorseful. To her it was only unvarnished truth.

He gently grasped her tiny face with his big weathered hand, turned her head to examine the darkening eye. Tried to steady the racing of his heart. "Why, baby? Why?"

"She said I smelled like bait."

Sean's gaze dropped to the miniature boots Alex seldom removed—the ones he'd had custom-made to match his own. "Our boots do smell like bait, sweet pea. So what was the real reason you hit her?"

Alex's self-assurance wavered. Her chin wobbled and her shoulders sagged. "She…said…you must be a crummy dad if I had to go out lobstering to take care of you." Tears glistened in her eyes. "You're not a crummy dad. You're the best."

"Oh, honey." He pulled her into his arms.

She was fierce, his daughter, fierce and proud and loyal far beyond her age and size. A chip off the old McCabe block.

"Ahem." Candace Simmons, the school principal, appeared in the doorway to her office.

Sean stood. "Candace—" He caught himself. "Ms. Simmons."

"Mr. McCabe." She looked as if she didn't relish either the necessary formality or the task at hand. "I'm afraid we have a zero-tolerance policy toward fighting. As I told you on the phone, Alexandra is suspended from school. For two weeks."

"You said she'd be suspended for one." He recognized the need for punishment, but two weeks was harsh.

"That was before Alexandra produced this from her boot." Candace held out a letter opener Sean recognized as a freebie for taking out a loan at the

Ocean National Bank. It had a faux scrimshaw whale for a handle. "We also have a zero-tolerance policy toward weapons."

"Alex?" A headache forming behind his eyebrows, Sean looked at his daughter for an explanation.

"It's not a weapon, Dad. I carry it in case of snake bite."

"You know perfectly well there are no poisonous snakes at Pritchard's Neck Elementary." Sighing deeply, Candace turned to Sean. "It's this inability to distinguish reality from fantasy that gets your daughter in trouble."

"Clearly, she didn't intend to hurt anyone with the letter opener or she would have used it during the fight." He believed children should accept responsibility for their actions, but he also knew Alex. "She might fight, but she doesn't fight dirty."

"Sean." Candace spoke softly, but looked him right in the eye. "The rules are there for the safety of the children. Even if I wanted to, I can't make exceptions where safety is concerned. So…one week for fighting. One week for possession of a potential weapon. Two weeks suspension."

"But there are only two weeks left of school."

"Yes. The maturity Alexandra shows in completing her work outside of class will affect our decision to promote her…or not."

"You're telling me she might not pass?" Sean felt his blood pressure rise. "Hey, she's one bright kid."

"We both know that." Candace's pause spoke volumes. "But she's disruptive. She has tremendous difficulty staying on task. Difficulty, too, interacting with her peers."

"You know she's used to being around adults." Mainly because he was raising Alex in the home he shared with his father and his brother. "There's nothing wrong with that."

"Of course not. But Alexandra's behavior is beginning to hinder her education." Candace rested her hand gently on Alex's head. "When you take her to her pediatrician to look at that eye, please, discuss her classroom behavior."

"What are you suggesting?" Defensive, he slipped his arm around his daughter.

"I'm saying that there are sometimes physical reasons for behavior patterns." Candace's expression softened. "It's just wise to check."

"You're talking hyperactivity—drugs to counteract it?"

"You know that, by law, I can't make a medical diagnosis."

But she could push him in that direction, he thought, his jaw set. He would not drug his child. His active, inquisitive, normal child.

"In the meantime," Candace continued, "these

are the class assignments for the rest of the year." She handed Sean a hefty packet. "I'll personally monitor Alexandra's suspension but she'll need adult supervision at all times."

"Of course." Taking Alex's hand, Sean stood, feeling as if they were two against the world.

Under the best of circumstances, Alex required almost constant supervision. Unfortunately, Sean's circumstances weren't the best at the moment. In addition to pulling his own traps, he was building a lobster pound with his father and brother, a potential family business they'd laid their life savings on and had hoped to have up and running before school's end. Until the start of summer day camp, school had been Sean's only viable child-care option.

This suspension also brought home the hard fact that the time had come to rein in his adventuresome daughter.

Before Jilian had died, Sean had made her a solemn promise to keep their baby safe, but with each passing year the task grew more difficult. Especially with a child like Alex, who never colored inside the lines.

CHAPTER ONE

DID SHE HAVE THE STAMINA to spend one more minute in this town, a town that had essentially drop-kicked her from the nest?

As thunder rumbled in the distance, Kit Darling lifted the hair off the back of her neck and prayed for a breeze, a breath of fresh air, any movement at all to break the unusual June heat of this strength-sapping afternoon.

Rain would be a welcome relief. Rain would mean she could close down her stupid yard sale.

"How much is this?" A woman held up an over-size velvet painting of Elvis draped in a skimpy toga. Her companion, a second woman, snickered.

"The tag says five bucks," Kit snapped. She knew neither woman had any intention of buying the painting, or anything else for that matter. Knew they'd only come to gawk at her mother's tacky things and gossip about Cynthia "Babe" Darling, the woman who'd run off with Millicent Crenshaw's husband, leaving chaos, recriminations and a pile of unpaid bills in her wake.

Turning her back on the two women, Kit stalked to the shade of Babe's sagging front porch and tried to turn her thoughts to the weather. Anything other than the woman who was her mother in name only.

Why didn't it rain? And wash away the ghouls who'd come to pore over the leftovers from Babe's sorry life.

Kit hated the overt cheesiness of her mother's possessions. The erotic paintings. The tasseled, satin pillows in garish colors. The hundreds of candles with fragrance like Naked Lunch and Lusty Musk. Items Babe had bought to enhance her femme fatale image, now spread over the yard in an attempt to take a bite out of her mother's debts, since it was her unfortunate responsibility to pay them. Kit hated Babe for sucking her back to the hometown she'd discarded nine years ago. The hometown that had discarded her years before that.

Responding to a flash of heat lightning in the distance, the two women, the only customers left in the dusty front yard, scurried to their car.

Good riddance. Kit might need the money, but she sure didn't need the spotlight. Rumors of Babe's latest outrage had spread like a virus through this insufferable burg. People had flocked to the yard sale to see if the rumors were true. If Babe had indeed flown the coop, her little love nest.

Would she ever be able to claw her way out from under her mother's reputation? she wondered bitterly. Not in this town.

Nursing a powerful thirst, Kit bent to open a cooler on the porch step—the utilities in Babe's rented house had been cut off—when a movement in the shrubbery near the end of the porch caught her eye.

"You got any books?" A small child emerged from behind a wilted hydrangea.

Despite the heat, the kid wore rubber boots and a faded flannel shirt tucked into much-worn overalls. Her hair—on second glance, Kit could see it was a little girl—looked as if it had been combed with an electric mixer. Strands stuck to a face so grimy and sweat-streaked, Kit almost overlooked the black eye. A scrapper for sure, this newcomer couldn't be more than five or six.

Kit felt an instant affinity for the kid. She herself had been a scrapper.

"What's your name?" she asked, stepping off the porch.

"Alexandra Melinda McCabe. But my dad calls me Alex." The child looked her straight in the eye. "You got any books?"

Alexandra Melinda McCabe. The McCabes were an upstanding family in Pritchard's Neck. Which one of them didn't know better than to let a little kid run loose? And why wasn't the child in school on a Tuesday? "What grade are you in?"

"Three." She was small for her age.

"Why aren't you in school, Alex?"

"I got 'spended. For fighting." Alex rammed her tiny fists on her hips. "That's three questions I answered. Now, you. You got any books?"

"No. I'm sorry. I have books in my apartment in Boston, but not here." Babe had never been a reader. Men were her hobby. With Ed Crenshaw, she'd begun to specialize in younger men.

"Where are your parents?" Kit turned the conversation back to Alex.

"My dad's working."

Kit never failed to feel a stab of empathy when she saw a young child on the street, unsupervised.

"So your dad leaves you by yourself while he's working?"

"My Aunt Emily's watching me."

Kit glanced up and down the street. "I don't see her."

"She's gonna have a baby. She's lying down 'cause she can barely walk." Alex shot Kit a don't-push-your-luck look. "You ask as many questions as Ms. Simmons did before she 'spended me."

Kit suppressed a smile. She liked this kid. Liked her forthright manner and unconventional clothes. Her grime and her grit.

"You'd better head home before your aunt worries about you." She opened the cooler. "It's hot. Want a soft drink to take with you?"

Before Alex could answer, a pickup truck came to a sliding halt at the end of the driveway.

"Alex!" A big, dark-haired man leaped out of the driver's side, scowling. "Your Aunt Emily's been worried sick about you," he barked as he charged up the driveway. "She called me at the pound to say you'd disappeared. You were supposed to stay in her yard." His anger rolled before him like breakers on the beach.

Standing firm before his wrath, Alex pointed at the yard sale sign listing on its stake. "I saw the sign and came down for just a minute, Dad. To see if there were any Seafaring Cecil books."

Kit pricked up her ears at the mention of Seafaring Cecil. But she hesitated to speak, cautious about coming between the man and his daughter.

"Alex—" the father's anger quickly abated, replaced by weariness evident in the tiny lines fanning the corners of his eyes "—how could you see the sign if you weren't already halfway down the street?"

Alex fumbled in the pocket of her overalls. "With this." She retrieved a folding telescope Kit recognized as one of the offerings on Seafaringcecil.com.

The man seemed torn between exasperation and relief.

"She's only been here a couple minutes," Kit offered. "She told me she needed to get back. So as not to worry her aunt."

Alex flashed her a grateful look.

As the man turned his attention to Kit for the first time, she sucked in her breath. She would know those dark eyes anywhere.

He held out a hand. "Sean McCabe."

Oh, yeah.

Back when they'd gone to high school together, he'd been the cream of the crop, both scholastically and athletically. Every girl with a hormone to her name had lusted after him.

And Kit had not been immune.

Once, right before graduation, Sean had unexpectedly asked her out. Once and only once. And even then, he'd stood her up.

Kit could have sworn he'd only asked her out as some locker-room bet. The guys were always trying to find out if she was as easy as her mother.

At the unpleasant memory, Kit stiffened, but extended her hand, nonetheless. "Kit Darling."

As his big, work-roughened hand enveloped hers, a flash of recognition crossed his face. One corner of his generous mouth twitched.

"Do you know this lady, Dad?" Alex tugged on her father's jeans.

Kit swallowed hard. No one in Pritchard's Neck had ever called her a lady. With one innocent question, this little girl managed to lay bare a vulnerability Kit didn't want exposed. Especially not to Sean McCabe.

"We went to school together, punkin." Sean spoke to Alex, but never took his eyes off Kit.

Could he possibly remember how he'd stood her up as if she hadn't mattered? He'd been such a big man on campus. So why was Mr. Most-Likely-To-Succeed standing before her now in a T-shirt, jeans and lobstering boots instead of pinstripes and wing tips?

Kit withdrew her hand from his, unwilling to admit, even to herself, that he still made her pulse race.

Standing surrounded by the castoffs of her mother's reckless life, Kit felt on display and unguarded in front of the one person in this podunk town she'd ever allowed herself to admire.

Suddenly, she couldn't breathe. She needed to wrap up Babe's affairs and hit the road before she was tarred—once again—with her mother's brush. But the problems she'd inherited from Babe required cash, and right now Kit had a cash-flow problem. She needed to stay in town long enough to liquidate what her mother had left behind to salvage her own credit rating. And to prove that at least, she, Kit, had character.

The clouds on the horizon had grown thick and

dark. An uncomfortable prickly tension charged the air.

Alex sensed something was going on between her dad and this lady with the cool name—Kit, like the adventurer Kit Carson—but Alex couldn't figure out what. Dad had said they'd gone to school together. He'd gone to school with lots of people in town, but he never looked at them the way he was looking at Kit.

Dad didn't pay much attention to looks and always urged Alex not to either. But it was hard not to with Kit. She had purply-red streaks in her hair, two gold hoops in her left eyebrow and a cool tattoo like a skinny vine on her upper right arm.

Maybe Dad was interested in the motorcycle Alex had seen parked around the side of the house. When she and Dad read their adventuring books and planned their trips, they talked about how they'd get there. Alex always picked a motorcycle, and Dad eventually said okay—because it was all just pretend. This lady rode a motorcycle for real. Red. Like her cowboy boots. It was Alex's favorite color. The color of the travel lines she and Dad drew on their maps.

A big raindrop fell on Alex's head.

Her father put his hand on her shoulder. "Let's get moving, scout."

More raindrops fell. Alex glanced at all the stuff

spilling over the front yard, then at Kit. Her eyes had a squinched-up look. Like she was trying hard not to cry. Or scream. Alex would scream, too, if her things were about to get ruined.

The rain began to hammer on the porch roof.

"Dad, we gotta help put away!"

She wasn't sure he would. Though he'd do anything for his family and friends, he was real standoffish with strangers. But Kit wasn't a stranger. Dad had said they'd gone to school together.

"Please, Dad!"

"Not necessary!" Kit cried out as she kicked off her boots and dashed out into the yard barefoot. She looked mad as she hauled a nearby box full of shiny pillows out of the rain and onto the porch. Like maybe she hated all this stuff. Or the rain. Or Dad.

No way! Everybody liked Dad.

Alex pulled on his hand. "Puh-leeeese!" She suddenly needed Kit to like her dad, too.

"Okay," he said, his voice real rough and funny sounding. "I owe Kit one."

Now, what did that mean? Sometimes Alex did not understand grown-ups.

Reluctantly, Sean followed Kit into the rain.

Kit Darling.

The last person he expected to find his daughter hanging with. Damn. Alex had enough wild ideas of her own without picking up pointers from Kit.

Still, he'd heard the rumors. This yard sale had to hurt her pride. Big time.

And…he did owe her one.

He picked up a card table loaded with half-burned candles and headed for the porch, passing behind Kit who wrestled unsuccessfully with a stationary bicycle. Putting the table down, he went to help her.

"Go away!" she snarled, rounding on him like a cornered alley cat. A stray with attitude.

So, she didn't want him here. He opened his mouth to call Alex. Started to turn his back on Kit, whose claws-bared approach to life had always made her more enemies than friends.

But her makeup did him in.

The rain sluiced down her face, making the heavy black mask she'd drawn around her eyes run in a muddy mess. She reminded him of Alex the day she'd fallen off their wharf at low tide. Covered by gray muck, his daughter had been mad as all get out. Mad laced with scared and fragile.

Sean knew for a fact Kit wasn't fragile, but that childlike, smeared face, those enormous gray eyes got to him just the same.

Moved, Sean reached into his pocket for a clean handkerchief, then tried to wipe away the black goop streaming down Kit's face.

With lightning-quick reflexes, she grabbed his

wrist before the handkerchief touched her skin. "Don't," she growled, her small white teeth bared. "I'm fine. Just the way I am."

And she was. She looked like some ancient warrior princess, done up in battle paint, too young to defend her honor and her turf, but willing to fight to the death in the attempt.

"I know," he conceded, pulling his hand away and pocketing the handkerchief. "You always were."

Nine years ago he'd found her fascinating. The wild child of a wild child. Buried in responsibilities, he'd watched as Kit cut a swath of anger and anarchy through the school and community.

In their senior class, she'd been fifteen years old to his eighteen, having skipped twice. That didn't help make her popular.

She'd refused to sit for senior portraits, and someone on the yearbook staff had cruelly printed under the blank space that should have been Kit's photo, "Most likely to self-destruct by age twenty-one."

Kit had taken matters into her own hands. She'd ripped up her yearbook and left pages as calling cards wedged in the lumps of manure she'd dumped on and in the cars of the high-school principal, the yearbook adviser, the class president— Sean—the head cheerleader—Jilian, his girl—and a host of others Kit had obviously considered her tormentors.

He'd admired her guts.

By the time a school administrator knocked on Babe Darling's door, Kit had left town. At fifteen. Without waiting to collect her diploma.

Sean hoisted the stationary bike out of the mud and onto the porch, savoring Kit's stunned expression.

Only to meet the equally astonished gaze of his daughter. Alex stood on the porch, her arms wrapped around a bunch of soggy stuffed animals, cheap carnival prizes. The look she gave him saw right through him. She'd seen how he'd lost himself in this woman.

This would never do. Kit wasn't any part of his plan to keep his daughter safe.

"It's coming down bad, squirt." Affecting a nonchalance he didn't feel, he stuck his hand out into the river of rain running off the gutterless porch roof.

Alex plunked the stuffed animals onto the uneven flooring. "This is just like the time Seafaring Cecil was in Hong Kong and the vegetable seller's sampan sank. Cecil didn't leave till he'd helped get all the stuff out of the harbor. Remember, the guy was so grateful he gave Cecil a duck to roast?"

Sean chuckled.

Alex whooped and jumped off the top step into the yard. Her boots created splashes that reached her tiny waist as she made a beeline for a lamp molded in the shape of a naked woman.

"Are you two crazy?" Kit cried, racing up the steps with an ugly painting of an almost-naked Elvis. The velvet background was so wet and whorled, Elvis looked pitifully cowlicked. "Why are you still here?"

"Because it seems pretty damned important to you to save this stuff."

She looked at him as if no one had ever taken into consideration what was important to her.

At that moment Sean wanted to tell her he was sorry for standing her up nine years ago. It hadn't been at all the way she must have imagined. But, he couldn't give in to the attraction he'd always harbored for her. He needed his parenting wits about him, and Kit, he felt sure, had the potential to drive him witless.

"Hey, look at this!" Alex bounded back up onto the porch, carrying a plastic laundry basket full of Hollywood fan magazines. "It was sticking out of the bottom." Nearly bursting with excitement, she took out a scrapbook. "It's full of stuff about Seafaring Cecil."

There were clippings about the gonzo travel writer's adventures, his interactive Web site and the merchandise his adventures, site and books had spawned.

Alex turned to Kit, her eyes sparkling. "If this is part of your yard sale, I wanna buy it!"

Kit looked overwhelmed. "I…I…don't know."

"Is it yours?" Alex persisted.

"It must be my mother's," Kit replied. The rain drummed on the porch roof as her fingertips hovered over the scrapbook. "I never knew she took any interest in me."

"You?" Alex flipped through the pages. There were no photos of the intrepid fisherman-traveler. "This is about Seafaring Cecil."

"I know, kid." Kit looked squarely at Alex. "I'm Cecil. It's my working name."

CHAPTER TWO

ALEX COULDN'T STOP grinning. Could the lady in front of her really be Seafaring Cecil? The man—no, the person—who'd traveled the seven seas and a few rivers thrown in for good measure? The person who'd eaten stir-fried bugs and drunk snake's blood? The person who'd helped Dad and her plan their ultimate-awesome-when-they-won-the-lottery trip?

Funny, but Kit looked just as cool as Alex had imagined Cecil to be. Only he was a lady.

Still, her dad had taught her not to believe everything people told you.

Crossing her arms over her chest, she looked up at Kit and issued her challenge. "Prove it."

Give her credit, Kit didn't back down. "Did you ever look at the copyright page in any of the books?"

"Nope." Alex shook her head. "We always got right to the good stuff."

Kit smiled and Alex noticed her front tooth was

just the tiniest bit crooked. She imagined it got that way when Kit had to open her emergency rations with her bare teeth. Maybe. It could happen. Cecil didn't live like ordinary people.

"If I had a book here," Kit said, "I could show you. It would say, 'Copyright by Kit Darling.' Me."

A brilliant idea popped into Alex's head. "We have Seafaring Cecil books at our house. Every one." She tugged on her dad's pocket. "Can Kit come to supper tonight? We could check it out then."

Dad looked like he'd been turned to stone with a voodoo curse.

"That's okay." Kit was acting funny, too. She probably wasn't used to eating at a table with knives and forks. "I should be making supper for you. For your help. But I'm fresh out of duck for roasting. Plus the utilities are off." She gave Alex a wobbly smile.

Alex felt a stab of disappointment. "I should have known a big shot like you wouldn't—"

"Hey, it's not like that. I'm no big shot." Kit knelt before her on the porch. The rain all around made it feel like they were marooned in the middle of the jungle. In Brazil maybe. Or Thailand. Up close, Alex got to look at Kit's cool vine tattoo. Had a rain forest tribesman given it to her?

"I'm only in town for a short while," Kit explained. "I have a long list of appointments. Lawyers, mostly." She made a face. "Then I need to get back on the road again. New places to visit. New things to write about." She looked kinda sorry. "But I do want to thank you for your help. And for being a Cecil fan. Perhaps tomorrow you could bring me your books and I'll autograph them. We could have a picnic lunch on the boulder out back while your dad's working. It would give your aunt a break."

Alex held her breath, looking at her dad. He cleared his throat.

"I don't think so," he said. Sean had pinched lines between his eyes. Like he had a stomachache. "You see…Alex has been suspended from school for two weeks. The suspension doesn't include picnics."

Now why did he have to bring that up? Just when she was about to make friends with Seafaring Cecil.

Kit inwardly cringed at the reluctance she heard in Sean's voice. Of course he wouldn't want his daughter associating with her. Kit the Pariah. In full view, at Babe Darling's. Mother Pariah. Without her pseudonym, she was still a Darling. One of two town outcasts.

"I understand." For Alex's sake she wouldn't make a scene. She smiled at the little girl with the big spirit. "You check that copyright page when you get home."

She extended her hand to Sean, determined to

show him his brush-off didn't faze her. "Thanks. For your help."

"Seems like you could use more," Alex offered. "I could come down tomorrow and help you spread this stuff out to dry." She stared up at her father. "That would be community service, Dad. Not a picnic."

Kit looked around at Babe's soggy possessions, now mostly piled on the front porch. She didn't know if anything was salvageable, if it ever had been in the first place.

"What are you planning to do?" Sean asked, his voice brusque and his body poised to get the heck out of Dodge.

Kit glanced at him. She didn't like the look in his eyes. Pity, maybe? She didn't need anyone's pity, least of all his.

"I'll just call a junk man to haul it all off," she declared airily. Maybe a junk man would give her something for the lot. Seafaring Cecil had only recently begun to make a real, if modest, living for Kit. She didn't have a cushion to soften the fallout from her mother's defection. "Yeah. A junk man."

"See." Sean looked at his daughter. "All taken care of."

Kit got the impression he wasn't only speaking of Babe's junk.

Alex seemed unconvinced, but she remained

silent. An interesting kid. There was more to her than met the eye.

The downpour stopped as quickly as it had begun, leaving the yard awash in mud. The few stray belongings they'd failed to retrieve and the yard sale sign had been swept into the street. There was nothing to keep Sean McCabe and his daughter any longer, and Kit felt an unexpected and unwanted twinge of disappointment.

She tried to shrug it off by picturing an adoring wife and mother waiting for them back home. His high-school sweetheart perhaps. The one he'd stood her up for.

"Come on, Alex." Sean put his hand protectively on the back of his daughter's neck. "We have to check in with Aunt Emily. Then I'm taking you to the pound where Pop and Uncle Jonas can help me keep an eye on you."

And where was the wife? Kit wondered, forced to remind herself she didn't care.

Sean made a move toward the porch steps, landing on one of the cowboy boots Kit had kicked off earlier. There wasn't much maneuverability in the heavy boots he wore and he grabbed at the rickety railing. It gave way under his weight. In seconds, he toppled backward off the porch and into the rain-drenched hydrangea.

"Dad!" Alex shrieked and flew off the porch,

landing in the muddy front yard. She lost her foot-
ing, too, and slid down the sloping yard.

Kit didn't know where to help first until Alex
sat up with an enormous mud-spattered grin. Sean,
however, lay flat on his back.

As quickly as she could without becoming a ca-
sualty herself, Kit made her way down the two
shallow front steps barefooted. If she weren't so
concerned that he'd broken or ruptured something,
she might find the situation funny.

Mud oozing between her toes, she slipped, then
fell to her knees. She crawled the rest of the way
to Sean. "Are you all right?"

"My ego's shot to hell," he muttered. Flat on his
back and vulnerable, he looked far sexier than up-
right and in charge. He glowered at the offending
red cowboy boot that teetered on the edge of the
porch. "That nearly killed me."

Gingerly, Kit stood, dug her bare feet into the
mud, then extended her hand.

He eyed her doubtfully.

"I'll help!" Alex materialized at Kit's side.

Taking a hand each, Sean braced his boot heels
in the mud.

"One, two, three!" Alex crowed.

They pulled as he heaved himself out of the
bush, slamming against Kit. Gleefully, Alex danced
away as the two adults fell once again.

Before they hit the ground, Sean grabbed Kit to him and rolled to his side. They slid like two harbor seals in a long mucky embrace down what once was—a very long time ago—a lawn. The wind knocked out of her, Kit couldn't move, although she hated to think of the shape she'd be in if Sean hadn't broken their fall—her fall—by flipping to his side. Pancake came to mind.

She felt the corded strength of his arms around her, felt the rise and fall of his rock-hard chest. Heard his ragged breathing and something else…something strange. The low, rusty beginnings of a laugh. The crinkles around his eyes told her she wasn't mistaken. Holding her tightly, he threw back his head and roared. His teeth flashed stark white against his mud-daubed face.

His laughter proved infectious.

Return to Pritchard's Neck had put Kit on edge, and the man who now held her hadn't eased her sense of unbalance. This unintended pratfall pushed her over the brink. She flung back her head and gave herself over to a marvelous belly laugh as Alex performed a noisy dance around the two fallen adults.

"You're a sight." A broad grin lighting up his face, Sean brushed a clump of hair from Kit's eyes. His mud-slick fingertips raised goose bumps on her flesh.

"No one's about to ask you to tea at the Ritz," she replied, picking a hydrangea blossom from behind his ear.

He caught her wrist, his merriment transferred into longing. A shiver of reciprocal desire ran down her spine.

"Alex! What are you doing?" A woman's voice rang out with crisp authority.

Alex froze.

A look of horror on his face, Sean released Kit, and struggled to get up.

"Who's she?" Kit asked as he helped her up. The woman wore a neat business suit and was standing beside a sedan, her arms crossed. She did not appear amused by what she saw.

"Candace Simmons," Sean replied. He had the look of a schoolboy caught smoking behind the gym. "Alex's principal. And my sister-in-law's best friend."

When the woman recognized Sean, her face registered disappointment. Slowly, with a long glance at Kit, she got in her car and drove away. And Kit saw her chances of getting out of town without starting any new rumors evaporate like fog before the morning sun.

"HOW COULD YOU?" Nine months pregnant and an-grier than a hornet in a car wash, Emily McCabe leaned against her front door, her hands supporting her back. She stared at the two mud monsters. "How could you?"

Sean had stopped to tell his sister-in-law he'd found Alex and was going to take her to the lobster pound with him. Unfortunately, Candace had come and gone before them with the news of the spectacle in Babe's front yard.

"Alexandra, do you have any idea how worried I was when I couldn't find you?" Emily pushed a strand of lank hair out of her face. "Do you know how difficult it is for me to get around to look for you?"

"Yes'm." Alex scuffed one toe of her boot against the other. She didn't look at all sorry, Sean thought.

With difficulty, Emily knelt before Alex. "Honey, you scared me. If anything had happened to you..."

Sean felt guilty. He shouldn't have bothered his sister-in-law in the first place, but he'd nowhere else to turn for child care. His sister, Mariah, was working overtime at the local landscape nursery to pay for night school. Pop and Jonas were working above and beyond their regular carpentry jobs to get the lobster pound open before the tourist season peaked. His oldest brother, Nick, and his family were in the process of moving back to Pritchard's Neck, but they wouldn't be settled in until the end of next month. Brad's wife, Emily, had seemed Sean's only choice.

Emily and Brad's twins, Nina and Noah, were eight, and Olivia was six, which meant that they were away at school all day. So Sean had promised Emily that Alex would entertain herself, would be no trouble at all. He'd gotten the first part right.

"Do you understand why I was so upset?" Emily's voice had lost its edge.

"Sorry." Hugging her aunt, Alex finally seemed genuinely repentant.

"Then right around to the back, young lady, and hose off at the outside tap while I talk to your father." Emily looked as if she wasn't going to let Sean get away as easily.

Alex trotted around the corner of the house, a tiny smile turning up the corner of her lips, obviously already imagining she was on her way to water some trusty safari animal.

"She didn't mean any harm," Sean offered.

"She never means any harm." Sighing, Emily smoothed the tent-like dress over her swollen form. "She's in her own little world without consequences. A world you give far too much encouragement."

"She saw the yard-sale sign down the street." Sean stopped himself. Emily looked as if her physical strength and emotional patience had run out with her pregnancy. She didn't need one more person challenging her. Not now, anyway. "She wanted to see if there were any books."

"Books." Emily rolled her eyes. "If it's not books, it's lobstering. If it's not lobstering, it's those wild travel fantasies you cultivate. Candace says Alex needs to focus more on—"

"I'm sorry she caused you grief." He didn't want to pick a fight with the woman who'd tried to do him a favor, but he didn't need yet another lecture on child rearing. He was doing the best he could.

"You need to nudge her in the right directions," Emily said gently. "Help her make more grounded choices."

"Are you saying I'm not a good role model?"

"Mud wrestling with Kit Darling in public…?"

"I wasn't mud wrestling."

"If you say so, but…Candace was devastated." Emily's shoulders sagged. "And I can understand why. She has Alexandra's best interests at heart. Yours, as well. And she has some expectations for her own."

"Don't go there, Emily. It was one dinner. A fix-up."

"You didn't give her a chance. She's still hoping—"

"Candace isn't my type."

"Oh, but Kit is?"

"Look. I found Alex with Kit. When the rain

started, Alex and I helped bring the yard sale stuff under cover. It was slippery. We fell. My eight-year-old happened to think it was funny."

"Funny! Two adults down on the ground, groping each other in the mud. One of them a single father and the other…the other trashy Babe Darling's daughter, no less."

"Would it have made any difference if I'd been mud wrestling with, say, Libby Fisk? Or Heather Abernathy? Or Candace Simmons?"

"Oh, Sean." Emily gave him a pitying look as if he were a lost boy. "All I want is for you to be happy."

"I'm happy enough."

"You know what I mean. I want you to have what Brad and I have. I want Alex to know a mother's love."

So did he, but finding the right woman for Alex—and for him—wasn't just an easy search on eBay. "I don't need a matchmaker, Em," he said as gently as he could.

"If this afternoon's any indication, I think you do."

"So we're back to Kit."

"I don't think she's…your type."

"I don't know what kind of woman Kit is," he admitted, keeping his tone even. "She hasn't been back to town in nine years. She claims to be a travel writer."

"Then she won't be staying. You need a woman who'll—" With one hand Emily grabbed Sean's arm. With the other she clutched her belly.

"What?" He knew without asking.

"It's time!" Emily gasped. "This is labor."

"Are you sure?" Had he and Alex precipitated this?

"Of course I'm sure!" Emily said through clenched teeth. "I've had three children. Oh—" Reaching into her dress pocket, she withdrew a cell phone and thrust it at Sean. "Call Emergency Response."

"I'll call Brad."

"There's no time!"

He punched in 9-1-1 and requested the Emergency Response Unit, then turned his attention to his sister-in-law.

"I need to sit," Emily pleaded, breathless.

As he helped her to the step, he tried not to think about Jilian's difficult delivery. "Can I do anything for you?"

"Yes!" She clutched his arm. "Promise me you'll see Candace tomorrow. Explain about this afternoon. She deserves an explanation."

Emily was right. Candace did deserve an explanation. Maybe even an apology. She was a good person. Just not the woman for him.

Another contraction almost doubled Emily over. Still, she clung to his arm. "Promise."

"I promise," he said quickly to alleviate her obvious distress.

Looking up, he saw a dripping Alex standing at the corner of the house, fear etched on her face.

"It's okay, punkin," he said, extending his free hand to her. "Aunt Emily's about to have her baby."

"Here?" Alex squeaked, running to him, throwing her wet arms around his leg.

Emily let out a short laugh. "You two adventurers would appreciate a front-yard delivery, wouldn't you?" She began to pant.

Sean put his arm around her and soothed her.

Within minutes the Emergency Response Unit arrived. Fortunately, the paramedics performed their duties seamlessly. Sean, with Alex plastered to his side, wouldn't have been much help. He assured Emily he'd wait for her children to get off the bus, that he would bring them to the hospital. He'd also get in touch with Brad. Yes, he knew his pager number.

As the paramedics began to close the doors to the unit, Emily caught and held his gaze.

"Let me call Uncle Brad," Alex chirped, patting the back pocket of Sean's jeans. "Hey! Where's your phone?"

With a sense of dread, he felt his empty pockets.

"It must have fallen out when you fell in the

mud. At Kit's." Alex's eyes lit up. "We'll have to go back to look for it."

"No." He didn't like that idea. "Not now. We can use Aunt Emily's."

Alex made a beeline for the phone abandoned on the front step. "But we'll have to get yours sometime," she declared with a grin. "And when we do, I'm bringing my books for Kit to autograph."

Sean's stomach dropped.

He'd thrown himself into Alex's fantasy of travel and adventure because it was only pretend. And, therefore, safe.

Then Kit blew into town. A real traveler with iconoclastic baggage. He didn't so much envy her travels as fear what she represented. She was the siren. Luring his daughter and enticing him with her song.

CHAPTER THREE

KIT SAT IN THE EMERGENCY ROOM cubicle, waiting for a nurse to return with her release forms. The stitched-up gash in her right forearm throbbed as the local anesthesia wore off. Biting her lower lip against the pain, she tapped the fingers of one hand into the palm of the other. It had been one long, frustrating day—starting with that blasted yard sale.

Sean and Alex McCabe had left her in a stew. Alex, because the kid reminded Kit of herself—or what she might've been like if she'd had the benefit of a remotely normal family. And Sean because...well, because Sean was Sean. Strong. Sexy. Self-confident. With an intriguing, barely suppressed anger—or an itch—that ran right below his responsible surface. He hadn't changed much in nine years.

Except now he had a daughter.

Did that mean he also had a wife? He hadn't been wearing a ring, but what lobsterman did? Around heavy equipment, a ring was a physical liability.

Why did Kit care about a ring or a wife?

Getting angry at herself for having given Sean McCabe's marital status two thoughts had been Kit's first mistake, she realized, thumping her heels against the examination table, waiting.

Hopping the neighbor's chain-link fence to use their backyard hose as an impromptu shower-and-clothes-wash-in-one had been her second. As she'd scoured reluctant grass stains out of her jeans with her fingernails, she had re-membered the feel of his body against hers. Re-membered the sound of his laugh. The look of intensity in his eyes as he'd explained why he'd stayed to help.

Because it seems pretty damned important to you.

Sean shouldn't have been her concern. Climb-ing back over the neighbor's chain-link fence should have been.

And that was her third mistake. Her thoughts unfocused, she'd slipped and ripped her forearm.

Where was that nurse?

Her skin crawled under her damp clothes, still dirty, while her stomach growled. It was seven o'clock. Breakfast and her morning shower at the turnpike truck stop were a distant memory.

A plump nurse with pastel scrubs and a tiny, fuzzy koala attached to her stethoscope entered the examination cubicle. Kit didn't know whether to resent Nurse Sunbeam's well-fed perkiness or envy her cleanliness.

"We've filed your insurance. Here's your release." She handed Kit a yellow sheet of paper, then a second white one. "And here are instructions for taking care of that wound. If you have any problems, don't hesitate to come back in."

"I won't have any problems," Kit declared, sliding off the examination table. She'd been in worse situations without benefit of hospitals and antibiotics. Her stomach growled again. She needed to find the cafeteria. Clutching her papers, Kit headed for the elevator.

The elevator doors opened onto a bright and cheery food court. Just as Kit stepped out, a doll's head rolled to a stop at her feet.

"Uncle Sean," a child complained, "Alexandra's not playing nice."

How many Seans and Alexandras could there be in Pritchard's Neck?

"But playing house is soooo boring," a now familiar voice shot back. Alex McCabe's. "I wanna play headhunters and cannibals."

"Eeuuww!" girlish voices chorused in disgust.

Kit picked up the doll's head.

Two little girls huddled on a plastic chair and tried to protect their family of dolls from a sword-wielding assailant. Make that a rolled-up newspaper-wielding assailant. Alex. Still dressed in mud-spattered overalls.

So where was her father this time?

A groan near a bank of soft-drink machines drew Kit's attention to two jean-clad backsides—one adult, one child—which presented themselves to the world from an ignominious position on the floor. It seemed the two were trying to retrieve something from under one of the machines.

"Aha!" Rolling to a sitting position, Sean held aloft a plastic action figure. "Look, Noah," he said, ruffling the young boy's hair and handing him the toy, "just because Alex dares you to do something, doesn't mean you have to—"

Sean stopped as if stung. Stopped and stared at Kit. The flinty look in his eye said she was the last person he expected—or wanted—to see.

Well, he was the last person she wanted to see.

"Kit!" Alex's face, on the other hand, transformed with joy. Throwing down the newspaper sword, she rushed at Kit as if to hug her, then pulled up short when she spied the bandage on her forearm. "What happened? Lions? Tigers? Bears?"

"No wildlife." Kit smiled. "A chain-link fence."

Sean rose stiffly to his feet. He hadn't managed a clean change of clothes either since they'd shared a mud bath. "You should get that arm looked at."

"Well, duh, Dad!" Alex rolled her eyes. "She's in a hospital. I think she already has."

Sean's ears turned pink as the three other children, now seated around a table littered with the remains of a meal, stared wide-eyed from Alex to Kit to Sean.

"We're waiting for Aunt Emily to have her baby." Alex seized Kit's uninjured arm. "Come meet my cousins."

Kit had never met anyone who accepted her so unconditionally, who championed her so exuberantly as Alex did.

"Maybe Kit was on her way somewhere, scout," Sean cautioned, as if he wished Kit would take off. The hungry look in his eyes, however, belied his gruff tone. "Let her be."

The corners of Alex's mouth turned down.

"I'd like to meet your cousins," Kit replied, slipping her hand into Alex's. She tried to ignore Sean's inhospitable words and her empty stomach. A round of introductions was the least she could do for the little girl who so openly accepted her.

Sean watched his daughter lead Kit toward Nina, Noah and Olivia.

"Hey, guys! Meet Seafaring Cecil." Sean winced at the hero worship in her voice.

His daughter loved new words, but he didn't know if she understood the meaning of transience. As in Kit's life. The McCabes were a rooted lot.

They might venture out on the tide, but they came back in on it as well. How would his daughter feel when Kit eventually took off—as she would, oh, yes, she would—without a backward glance?

"So tell them about your favorite trip," Alex insisted, clearly intent on showing off her prize.

It surprised Sean that his daughter had to draw Kit out. He would have expected more swagger from Seafaring Cecil. From a woman who'd hit the road at fifteen. But she stood, holding Alex's hand, and looked almost shy.

"My favorite trip is one I've never taken." She smiled and her smile was sweet and far away. "Kathmandu."

Could it be? Kathmandu was the trip she and he had mapped back in senior year when they were supposed to be researching the effects of geography on the Russian revolution instead. Their mutual passion for the freedom travel promised was what had led him to ask her out.

She glanced at him, then quickly looked away, blushing. "So maybe you'd rather see some tricks I picked up from a street performer in Montreal."

"I like tricks!" six-year-old Olivia chimed in. "But not mean ones."

"Can you saw a person in half?" Alex asked, her uninjured eye saucer-large.

"No tricks that complicated." Kit winked. "But

I can juggle and do card tricks and read palms and pick pockets—"

"Pick our pockets!" Alex exclaimed as the children leaned forward as one.

Slapping her hands over her miniature backpack, eight-year-old Nina appeared shocked. "Do you keep what you take?"

"No, no!" With a predatory feline grace Kit moved around the small group. "This is just for fun."

Her twin brother, Noah, danced from foot to foot, but Nina wore a pruney expression. "Picking pockets—"

Alex reached out and clamped her hand over her cousin's mouth.

"You've got to pick a pocket or two," Kit crooned, with a mischievous grin. "I give it all back afterwards to prove how clever I am. Cleverer than the people whose pockets I pick, whose belongings I snitch." Waggling her fingers, she looked into the children's eyes.

The kids giggled—except for Nina—and hugged their pockets.

"Who thinks they're cleverer than me? Who thinks they'd know if I fingered their valuables?" Kit twirled an imaginary mustache. At ease now. Lost in the game. Impish. And irresistible. "Who?"

"Me!" A spontaneous chorus of four. They were McCabes, after all. Sure of themselves.

When the hands shot up, Kit made her lightning quick move. Sean saw Olivia's bead bracelet disappear off her tiny wrist, noticed because Olivia had made such a big deal of finding that bracelet before coming to the hospital. Twisting to keep her eye on Kit, Olivia, however, seemed not to have felt a thing.

Sean examined Kit's moves more closely. Not an unpleasant task.

"Who thinks their young eyes are sharper than my old fingers?" she asked.

"Me!" The four craned their necks to keep their eyes on Kit prowling the perimeter of their rapt group.

As Nina wriggled uneasily, Kit slipped a bow from the cousin's hair, then palmed it out of sight. Nina didn't flinch, as the others squirmed and protected their own pockets.

Sean took note, however. He took note of every sensuous move Kit made. How the vine tattoo on her uninjured arm rippled over svelte muscle as Kit swiped then pocketed the children's little treasures. How intense and childlike her own expression turned as she wove a sense of magic with her voice and her movements. How her red cowboy boots clicked on the hospital's tiled floor as she moved around the group, holding their attention as a snake charmer would a snake.

In fact, he was so mesmerized that he failed to get out of her way on one of her turns. She bumped into him. Hard. But she wasn't hard. She might have the enthusiasm of a child, but she had the soft curves of a woman.

Patting him solicitously, she said, "Sorry."

He wasn't.

"You're all so clever," she remarked, returning her attention to the children. "A tough crowd. Protecting your pockets so well." She reached down and pulled a coin from behind Noah's ear. "I'll never put anything over on you." She held it up to the delighted giggles of her audience.

She handed the quarter to Alex. "Hold this between your hands." She adjusted Alex's hands to a prayer position, and his daughter's Seafaring Cecil compass ring instantly disappeared. "And I'll try to move Noah's money from here—" she tapped Alex's fingers "—to there." She tapped the pocket on Sean's shirt.

Her touch left a warm spot on his chest.

She threw her hands into the air. "Alakazam!"

Alex opened her hands, and the coin fell to the floor.

The group groaned its disappointment.

"You couldn't do it," Nina said, her face a stiff little smirk.

"But I could do this!" With a flourish, Kit held the pilfered goods aloft. One bead bracelet. One hair bow. One compass ring. And one very familiar wallet.

Sean's wallet. How the devil had she done that?

"Now who wasn't paying attention?" Kit crowed.

He'd seen her lift all the other stuff, but not his own. Obviously, that enjoyable bump she'd given him had scrambled his brain. She certainly had that power.

Alex rolled on the floor, her face contorted with glee.

"Well, I'll be—" Sean shook his head in admiration as Kit handed back his wallet.

"You need to keep a closer watch on your valuables, sailor," she murmured, a wicked gleam in her eye.

His pulse picked up.

Once Alex's cousins recovered, they erupted in a sea of demands.

"Teach me!"

"Teach me!"

"Teach me!"

"Is this a hospital, or did I make a wrong turn?"

Sean turned as his older sister, Mariah, marched off the elevator. She drilled such a look at Kit. Rude. His sister, a stunner and a spitfire who was completely overprotective of her younger brother Sean.

"Aunt Mariah!" Nina exclaimed. "Mom's having our baby."

"That's why I'm here, love." She bent down to

accept a group hug from the four cousins. "And guess what? I checked. There's a new kid on the block. Eric Aaron McCabe."

"Uncle Sean!" Noah whooped. "I got a brother!"

Alex stood on a chair and tossed impromptu confetti—shredded cafeteria napkins—into the air.

"Alexandra," Sean warned. "Get down and start cleaning up."

"All of you, chop, chop!" Mariah bustled about the table. "Help me clean up. As soon as Aunt Emily's back in her room, we can go up to see the baby." She turned to Sean, her back to Kit, her posture antagonistic. "Family only."

Sean thought it better to ignore her challenge. "I talked to Pop and Jonas. They'll be along as soon as they close up work on the pound."

"I think it would be better if we don't all descend at once on Emily," Mariah said. "After the kids have gone up, we can flip to see who takes the rug rats home for baths and bed." She cut a hard glance at Kit. "You've been here the longest, maybe you should take them home."

"I want to see our new baby," Olivia wailed.

"Brother," Noah insisted.

"I wanna stay right here." Alex thrust her skinny arm through Kit's shapely one.

Cocking one eyebrow, Mariah glared at Sean.

Sean refused to be intimidated. "Mariah, you remember Kit Darling. An old friend." Rebellion simmered in the half-truth. "Kit, my big sister, Mariah."

Mariah clamped her mouth shut, obviously reacting to rumors. She could be such a brat. Her brass made Sean want to shield Kit.

Kit shrugged. "I have to eat." Gently removing her arm from Alex's grasp, she handed back Olivia's bracelet, Nina's hair bow and Alex's ring. She flipped the coin to Noah.

"It's been real," she said, her voice suddenly tough. She let her hand rest for a moment on Alex's head. "You've been great."

Then, without so much as a glance in Sean's direction, she moved to the cafeteria's sandwich array.

And Sean, having wanted her to leave earlier, now desperately wanted her to stay.

Standing with her back to the lot of them, Kit paid for a ham on rye. Who the hell did Mariah think she was? Dishing out the cold treatment. Making Kit feel fifteen again. And lacking.

The only reason she hadn't decked the insufferable snot was because the insufferable snot was Alex's aunt. Alex deserved better.

She moved to the drink machines to purchase bottled water. But when she stuffed a dollar in the slot, the machine immediately spit the rumpled bill back at her. She banged the lit front with the flat of her hand.

"Lemme try." Alex stood next to Kit, empathy written on her face.

Kit handed her the dollar.

Carefully, as if the task were brain-surgery important, Alex straightened the kinks from the corners, then smoothed the entire bill by running it back and forth over the edge of the vending machine.

The gesture touched Kit. "Why are you being so nice to me?" she murmured.

Alex cocked her head, her gaze unwavering. "Because I like you." Simple as that. Yet not so simple when her family obviously wanted Kit out of their lives.

Kit glanced over her shoulder to where Sean and his sister were engaged in heated stage whispers. Nina, Noah and Olivia huddled near their aunt.

Kit looked back at Alex, a little person with an enormous heart. "I like you, too," she replied and felt pounds lighter for having admitted it.

Alex stuck the smoothed dollar in the slot, and the docile machine gave up a bottle of water. Scooping it out of the bin, she handed it to Kit.

"Thanks. Can I buy you one?"

"Alexandra," Mariah called over. "Come finish cleaning up."

The McCabes had always been clannish and tough as nails. They'd worn their hardscrabble respectability like a badge. The Darlings couldn't buy respectability with a bushel of money and a gold-plated plaque from the governor.

Kit turned on her heel for the elevator. To hell with them. All of them.

"Kit!" Alex called as the elevator doors slid open.

"Let her go, Alex," Mariah urged.

"Kit!" Sean called as she stepped into the car. "Wait!"

She punched the button for the lobby and felt an enormous sense of escape as the doors shut and the car began to descend, leaving Sean behind with his sanctimonious sister. Kit kicked the metal wall. Hard. Pain shot through her big toe.

In the lobby, she hobbled toward the entrance and the parking lot.

"Kit!" Sean had emerged from the second elevator.

She hobbled faster through the lobby's automatic doors and into the parking lot toward her motorcycle. Freedom on a kickstand.

But Sean's stride was too great. Catching up with her, he grasped her good arm and spun her around.

"Stop, dammit." His dark eyes burned into her. "Why are you running?"

Her heart raced in a rhythm all out of proportion to her brief sprint. Sean did her in with his smoldering eyes and push-me-pull-me looks. His yearning tinged with anger.

"Why aren't you inside with your family?" she demanded.

He held her arm as if he had every right to touch her. He didn't. Kit had fiercely guarded her right to tell a man when he could and when he could not touch her.

"Let me go," she growled.

He threw his hands in the air and took a step backward. "Not everyone in the world is the enemy, Kit."

"Tell that to your sister."

"She acted like a jerk. I apologize for her behavior."

"You owe me nothing."

"Ah, Kit…." A look of pain suffused his rugged features. "For a long time I've owed you an apology."

It was her turn to take a step backward.

"Back in school—"

She held up her hand to ward off what she realized was coming.

"In school," he continued, undeterred, "I asked you out, then stood you up." His words seemed scraped and raw. "I'm sorry."

She couldn't believe he'd brought that old hurt into the open.

"Why did you stand me up?" She pulled herself ramrod straight, prepared herself for his macho defense. Or, at the most, the admission of teenage stupidity. Peer pressure. Folding to a dare. "Why?"

"Jilian…" He cleared his throat. Clenched and

unclenched his hands. "Jilian told me she was pregnant. With Alex." His words sounded forced. "I wasn't thinking about anything or anyone else. We were married right after you left town."

Dumbfounded by this unexpected confession, Kit felt a stab of empathy for his wife. The gossips must've had a field day. "How would Jilian feel if she knew you were telling me this?"

In the light of the parking lot lamps, Sean's face appeared drained of all color. "Jilian's been dead six years. Car accident."

Kit didn't know what to say. She'd been prepared to stand up to him if he'd apologized for being a jerk. But this halting admission was too filled with pain.

"You didn't have to tell me all this."

"I did." He glowered at her as if he hadn't wanted to tell her anything. "Because you shouldn't think I wasn't attracted to you. Then."

He said *then*, but his eyes said *now*. She'd seen desire in men's eyes before. Lust. Crude and controlling. The look in Sean's eyes was different, tinged with vulnerability. Telling her the truth had cost him.

Unaccountably, tears stung her eyes.

"Kit..." He moved to draw her to him, kiss her maybe. She couldn't quite tell. His tenderness and unguarded yearning made her wild. She could have handled his scorn. Or his pity. But not this sensitivity.

Drawing back, she slapped his face with all her might. As much to punish him for arousing her deeply guarded feelings now as for his inadvertent cruelty all those years ago.

CHAPTER FOUR

HIS CHEEK STILL SMARTING from Kit's slap, Sean stepped out of the hospital elevator and into a Mc-Cabe celebration. With all the goings-on, surely his bruised ego would go unnoticed.

Pop and Jonas had arrived in the maternity floor waiting room and Brad was passing out cigars, both real and chocolate. The kids were wild from junk food, missed bedtimes and the adults' high spirits.

"Once he decided to come, there was no stopping him!" Brad exclaimed, his chest puffed out. "And he's a keeper, all right. Eric Aaron McCabe. Seven pounds, eleven ounces and eighteen inches of squalling testosterone."

Jonas clapped Brad on the back.

"He's right. I just saw him. And Emily looks great, too."

Mariah appeared around a corner. "I'll call Nick and Chessie," she said. "They'd better move back home quick before the selectmen declare Pritchard's Neck has its quota of McCabes."

"Hush, girl." Pop gave his only daughter a loving glance that belied his gruff reprimand. "There could never be enough of you to suit me." Penn had fathered five children. Now he counted on those offspring to build his dynasty.

A nurse appeared, and Sean recognized her as one of Pop's poker pals. "Visiting hours are over, and you need to let the new mom rest. But, if you can control yourselves, I'll bend the rules just the tiniest bit and let you take a peek at the new family member…who'd better have a good set of pipes to be heard over the lot of you."

"Ah, Adele," Pop crooned, affecting an Irish brogue. "I've a soft spot in me heart for a lass in uniform. Can I buy you a cuppa when your shift is done?"

Adele leveled Pop with a flinty glare. "You can pay your poker debts, Penn, and I'll call us even."

Her retort shut the older man up momentarily.

"Now," Adele continued, "if you can hold on for just a few more minutes, we'll have your baby ready for viewing in the nursery. But first, Emily would like to speak to you, Sean."

"Me?"

"You sure she wasn't asking for the proud grandpa?" Pop asked, feigning insult.

"I think I know the difference between you and your sons," Adele replied. "I'll be back for the rest of you when the baby's ready." She squinted at the assembled clan. "And try to keep your conversation to a dull roar."

With that, she set off down the corridor at a brisk clip, Sean in her wake.

"Did Emily say why she wanted to see me?" he asked.

"You can ask her yourself." The nurse stopped outside one of the rooms. "She's in here."

Emily was sitting up in bed when Sean came in, holding the baby and looking radiant.

"Do you want to hold your nephew?" she asked.

"You bet."

Sean took the tiny bundle and stared down in wonder at the newest family member. "Hey, I'm your Uncle Sean." The baby yawned, unimpressed. "He's a handsome dude, Em."

"Thank you. We think so." Emily shifted her pillow, cleared her throat. "Would you like to have more children?"

Yeah, he would. "I've got Alex," he said, concentrating on the infant in his arms. "And a whole lot of nephews and nieces. That's plenty."

"Family's important."

"Nothing more important."

Another nurse appeared in the doorway. "I'm here to take the baby. If we don't get him in the nursery soon, I'm afraid your family's going to riot."

"They're an impatient bunch." Sean chuckled as he handed Eric over. He turned to Emily. "I'd better let you get your beauty sleep."

"Just a minute," Emily replied. "I wanted to talk to you."

Sean shifted uneasily.

"I've been a McCabe long enough to know what a devoted father and family man you are, Sean. You deserve a woman with the same values."

"How did this get to be about me?"

"Mariah told me Kit was with you in the cafeteria."

"She wasn't *with* me. It was pure coincidence we ended up in the same room."

"Hmm. Two coincidental meetings in one day." Emily obviously didn't believe him. "Mariah said there was chemistry between you two."

"Mariah's got an imagination as vivid as Alex's."

"Alex is definitely attracted to her."

"Kit's not staying in town."

"Exactly. Why would you want to start up with someone who's leaving?"

"I think we've had this conversation."

Emily looked him in the eye. "My friend Elaine works for a consumer credit counseling service in Biddeford. The agency helps people manage their debt once they're in trouble. Kit paid them a visit to get help sorting out Babe's financial mess."

"I don't think Elaine should have told you this, and I don't think you should be repeating it to me."

Emily acted as if she hadn't heard. "It seems Kit cosigned with Babe on all her accounts. When Babe skipped town, she left Kit with thousands of dollars in debt. Thousands."

Sean cringed. What kind of person would do that to family? A mother putting that burden on a daughter was unbelievable. It was a betrayal. He thought of how implicitly he trusted Pop and Jonas and the deal they'd struck on the pound. Bailing out and leaving a family member stranded was so far outside Sean's realm of experience, he felt suddenly protective.

"You can't hold that against Kit," he declared. "She's trying to do what's right."

"I know," Emily said quietly. "I'm telling you this because I'm worried about you and Alex. For us, family ties, loyalty and reliability mean everything. For Kit…who knows?" She gave his hand an affectionate squeeze. "You're a good man, Sean. I don't want you to get hurt. I don't want Alex to get hurt."

"Neither do I. Good night, Em." He kissed his sister-in-law on the top of her head, unwilling to admit that she'd effectively made her point. He and Kit were worlds apart. "Don't worry."

He left the room to find his daughter.

Back in the waiting room, Alex sat alone in the corner, scowling and peeling the label off a soft drink bottle. Sean could hear the rest of his family down the hall, presumably admiring the baby in the nursery.

"Hey, june bug, don't you want to see your new cousin?"

Alex shrugged. "I dunno."

"What's wrong?"

"Why did Kit have to go?"

Sean sat beside his daughter and put his arm around her shoulder, fragile as a bird's wing. "Kit's not part of the family, hon. Besides, she finished her business at the hospital and headed home."

"So why'd you follow her?"

"I...thought Kit's feelings might be hurt. I wanted to apologize."

"Aunt Mariah wasn't real friendly to her."

"No, she wasn't." He chucked Alex under the chin. "Hey, sport, if you want to see Eric, we'd better get a move on."

Alex stayed put and crossed her arms over her chest. It was no secret she'd inherited his stubborn streak. "I like Kit."

"I know you do." He rubbed the back of his neck, massaged the tense muscles. "And she likes you. There's nothing wrong with that."

What was wrong was his inappropriate attraction to a woman who rocked his sense of responsibility. When she'd jumped on her motorcycle after slapping him, his first thought had been to climb on that powerful machine with her. He could imagine the evening breeze on his face, the heady sense of freedom, the thrill of not knowing what lay around the corner.

"I just wanna be her friend," Alex whispered, her face pinched in confusion. "I don't understand what's going on."

His child deserved the best explanation he could muster.

"When Kit lived here," he began, "she wasn't happy. She didn't make friends easily. She always wanted to leave, to see the world. She only came back because her mother messed up and Kit has to help her out. She's not happy about it, and she can't wait to leave. Alex, honey, it's hard to make friends with a person who has no intention of sticking around."

Sliding off the chair, Alex threaded her tiny fingers through Sean's big ones. "Maybe she'd stick around if she had friends."

It was hard to argue with a child's simple logic.

He didn't try. Instead, he led her down the corridor to where the rest of the family stood in front of the large nursery window, behind which the plastic bassinets were empty, except for one. It

seemed Eric Aaron had center stage to himself tonight in this small coastal hospital. Better he
should be in the spotlight than his Uncle Sean.

Lifting Alex up so she could see her new cousin,
a flood of memories washed over him. He'd stood
at this very window and gazed down at the pink
bundle he and Jilian would take home. Alex.

He felt a pang of guilt now, that he'd been less
consumed with love or awe at that time and more
worried about how two nineteen-year-olds and a
newborn were going to make it on their own.

Near the end of senior year, when Jilian had told
him she was pregnant, he'd had to turn down a
scholarship to Brown to do the right thing—to
promise to love, honor and cherish her. He'd managed the honor part, no sweat, and he'd worked on
cherish. But, regretfully, love came too late.

"So you're going to help your Uncle Jonas and
me work on the pound tomorrow while your dad's
pulling traps." Pop stood next to him, talking to Alex.

"Sorry, Pop Pop." Alex rubbed her eyes. It was
past her bedtime. "Seafaring Cecil's in town, and
she said I could help her. We're gonna get her yard
sale stuff ready for the junk man."

"Reality check." Sean set Alex firmly back on
the floor. "We talked about this earlier. You're to
stay with Pop Pop and Uncle Jonas and work on
your school assignments."

Alex covered her ears and closed her eyes.

"What's going on, skipper?" Pop ruffled Alex's hair. "You want to throw your grandpop over for some old travel writer?"

"She's not old." Scowling, Alex raised her voice. "She's cool. And she's only here for a little bit, and she promised to autograph my books."

The others turned as one, their attention diverted from the baby to Sean and Alex. Mariah shot Sean a what-have-you-gone-and-let-your-daughter-do-now look.

"Alex, enough." He pulled her hands from her ears. "You're overtired, and it's time for bed. We're going."

Alex yanked hard on his hand. *But I want Kit to watch me tomorrow! Not Pop Pop and Uncle Jonas!* She shouted so loudly, Eric let out a high-pitched yelp behind the plate glass.

"McCabes, out. Now." Adele stormed down the corridor.

"Sheesh," Noah muttered, slouching past Alex. "Why'd you hafta ruin it for everybody?"

Unabashed, Alex stuck her tongue out at her cousin.

Brad patted Sean on the back as he and Mariah herded his brood down the hall. "Hang in there, buddy."

"Hold the elevator." Trying not to grin, Pop followed.

"Be good." Jonas tweaked Alex's nose in passing. "See you tomorrow."

"Nuh-uh," Alex muttered almost inaudibly.

"What did you say?" Alone in the corridor, Sean knelt on one knee before his daughter.

Alex refused to speak. This was so unlike her. Normally, she told him far more than he needed to know. She didn't argue with him. And she loved spending time with Pop and Jonas.

Sean tilted her chin so that she had to look at him. "I won't have bratty behavior."

"I'm not a brat," Alex muttered.

"But you're behaving like one."

"Then you're behaving like one!" she wailed. "Seafaring Cecil's our favorite. But now she's right here, you won't let me be nice to her. You're just a big phony!"

"You've crossed the line, Alex. I won't tolerate disrespect."

"But everybody's disrespecting Kit!" she cried.

Sean gritted his teeth. "Kit is no concern of ours." She certainly wasn't if she could drive this ugly wedge between him and his daughter, between him and his family.

"But Daaaad—"

"Not a word, Alex. I mean it." Picking up his

daughter like a sailor's duffel, he headed for the elevator.

Alex withdrew into silence and became stiff in his arms, clearly showing her displeasure, clearly shutting him out.

SOMETHING WASN'T RIGHT.

Kit pushed open the front door to Babe's rental. She could have sworn she'd locked the tiny house. But then nothing worked in this place. The long Maine twilight cast the sparse furnishings in gloom, making them appear shabbier, if that was possible. Babe had always rented, and she'd always rented furnished. She used to say that as long as she had a springy double bed, she was home. She always told Kit things Kit knew other mothers didn't share with their daughters. Shouldn't share.

The faint odor of a man's cheap cologne hung in the air. Was it new—an unsettling thought—or just a lingering reminder of Ed Crenshaw?

Sean didn't wear cologne.

He smelled of the sea and of shirts hung out to dry in the tangy salt air. He smelled like a man who worked out-of-doors for a living ought to smell.

She moved her foot to feel for the backpack with her flashlight where she'd left it beside the front door. The pack and her sleeping bag were her only luggage. She traveled light.

Hairs rose on the back of her neck as she suddenly realized that her things had been moved from one side of the door to the other. Flattening herself against the wall, she listened intently. Nothing. Not a sound except crickets chirping beyond the front screen door.

Sliding slowly down the wall, she fumbled in the outer pocket of her backpack for her flashlight—weapons grade, she'd called it when she'd bought it—but didn't turn it on. She had a cell phone, but the battery was dead. Besides, who would she call? The police? She'd never considered the police on her side. No, the heavy flashlight would have to do.

She scanned her surroundings. The house was minuscule. Kit hadn't noticed—or felt—anything amiss when she'd clambered over the yard sale mess on the porch. The front door opened directly into a living space that elled on the left into a kitchen and eating area. In daylight she could see the entire area from where she stood. Her eyes now accustomed to the dusk, she detected no out-of-place shape or movement.

But she sensed something—or someone.

Straight ahead, the door to the single bedroom hung open. Kit could see most of the room, the double bed, the single dresser. She couldn't see into the bathroom off the bedroom or out onto the back porch, which opened off the kitchen. Never lifting her gaze from the bedroom doorway, she stood on one foot and then removed a boot. Prepared to flee out the front, she flung it with all her might through the bedroom doorway. The boot landed with a thud against the far wall, the noise echoing throughout the mostly empty house.

Nothing but the racing of her heart.

She slipped her foot out of the other boot, then crept barefoot across the living room into the kitchen. It, too, was empty and silent. She felt a little foolish, Kinsey Millhone in a Nancy Drew town.

Peering through the window over the kitchen sink, she couldn't see anything on the porch. She tried the back door. It was also unlocked. How many men had Babe given keys? Every sense alert, she stepped outside.

Twilight had receded into night, but the moon hadn't risen yet. The house was set back from the road in a thick copse of evergreens that hid the neighbors on either side and out back. Kit scanned the line of trees.

Off to the right, a few yards into the trees, was a huge granite outcropping. She couldn't see it now in the dark, but beyond the trees where the rocks were, a small glow caught Kit's attention. Too orange for a firefly, it was more like the lit end of a cigarette. As she stared, frozen, the light arced then disappeared.

Sometimes retreat was the better part of valor.

Kit backed into the house and locked the door, jamming one of the kitchen chairs under the knob. Hefting the other chair to the front door, she locked and jammed that too. There were only five windows in the entire house. She checked that they were all shut and locked. It would be stuffy, but in her travels she'd experienced stuffier. Physical discomfort barely registered on her sensory radar. Emotional discomfort…well, better not go there.

She grabbed her sleeping bag and unrolled it under the kitchen table. An intruder would least expect to find her there, although she hoped she was just being paranoid. Too much time spent in this stupid prying town.

An intruder? More likely kids, hearing the rumors of Babe's flight, had checked to see if the house was empty for a smoke or an illegal beer scarfed from Mom and Dad's fridge.

Kit quickly shed her jeans, then crawled on top of the sleeping bag in her tank top and panties. Lying under the table, she snorted softly at herself. She should have been wearing her cap-cam. Her Seafaring Cecil fans would have found a video version of this latest adventure a hoot. It would certainly blow her tough-guy persona.

She breathed slowly, trying to regain her center. Four slow breaths in, four out. She tried to focus on a pleasant memory—kayaking in Tasmania. But her mind wandered to Alex McCabe and her small kindnesses.

And thoughts of Alex led to thoughts of her father.

Those two were a package deal. Unfortunately, Aunt Mariah, the ice princess, came with the package, too. As well as all the other self-righteous, respectable Pritchard's Neck citizens.

Kit didn't need the Sean McCabe package deal.

She pressed the button on her watch, illuminating the dial. Ten o'clock. She might as well call it a day. Tomorrow she planned to get up at dawn, to tackle Babe's financial problems, and leave this town and its unsettling memories—and possibilities—as soon as she could.

RELISHING THE NIGHT QUIET, Emily stroked Eric's tiny head as he nursed contentedly beside her on the hospital bed. With Olivia, her second born, Emily had learned to appreciate the private time in the hospital when the family had gone and the nurses had turned down the lights on the ward. With Nina and Noah, she'd been overwhelmed by the excitement of being a new mother and the novelty of twins—and McCabes trying to sneak onto the floor after-hours. Brad, who would now have his hands full at home, had led the pack.

Yes, she savored this time alone with her new son.

The hectic return home would come soon enough. It wasn't that she didn't love being a McCabe. She did. But her husband's family was rough around the edges. Emily chalked up their sometimes unrestrained behavior to growing up motherless.

On that count, she'd been lucky.

She couldn't wait for the end of the month when her own mother and father would get back from their cruise through the Far East. They would simply dote on Eric as they did their other three grandchildren.

She was dying to visit them at their big oceanside house in Cape Elizabeth—she felt a little guilty still thinking of it as home.

One look at Brad's bouquet of long-stemmed roses, and Emily stifled her vaguely disloyal thoughts. She wouldn't trade her life with him for anything in the world. It hadn't been easy, but she'd learned to do without a housekeeper—or a cook. Or even a gardener. An only child, she'd wanted nothing more than to be a wife and mother of a large family. Brad's family was part of his attraction.

She gently pressed her finger to her breast near Eric's mouth, releasing the suction. My, but he had an appetite. Rolling on her back, she placed him on her stomach, belly to belly, then rubbed his back and reveled in his scent while waiting for that satisfying baby burp.

She was proud of Brad. A lineman for the electric company wasn't quite the son-in-law her parents had expected. Her mother had wanted Emily to marry a doctor as she had. But Brad was intelligent and a hard worker like the rest of his family—well, all except for Penn, a hail-fellow-well-met kind of guy, who maintained his status in town simply by having five great kids. And the night courses Brad took would eventually lead to a bachelor's and maybe even a master's degree. Emily hoped for an MBA, at least.

Until then, no one could ask for a more devoted husband and father. After four children, he still had the power to make her legs turn to jelly. She felt heat rise to her cheeks just thinking of how they'd met. At a rally in Portland to support state funding for school music programs. She'd played cello in her high school's symphony orchestra. He'd played trumpet in his school's jazz band.

The jazz band guys had all worn fedoras and forties-style suits and Brad had been a standout, both in looks and talent. Unable to take her eyes off him, Emily had begged her best friend to act as go-between and get an introduction. While the introductions still hung in the air, he'd asked her for a date.

The fireworks had started when Mother and Father found out Brad was from Pritchard's Neck. As if it were the end of the world. Well, it turned out to be the end of Emily's world as she'd known it. Her squeaky clean, protected world.

She hadn't understood her parents' reaction until she had her own children and felt that overwhelming need to protect them.

From people like Babe Darling.

Emily couldn't quite understand why Babe upset her so much. Scared her even.

Her parents had sheltered her, perhaps too much. Brad still sometimes teased her about how naive she'd been when they'd met. But she'd grown up fast after marrying young—right after high school graduation—and having children quickly.

While she hated to see Sean lonely—and he was, even if he wouldn't admit it—and Alex growing up wild and motherless, she was worried he would make a stupid, life-altering decision. Candace Simmons would be perfect for them.

Kit Darling would not.

Eric burped softly.

"There's my little man," Emily crooned. She turned and positioned him to nurse on her other side. Motherhood and family were her universe. And she needed to be vigilant to protect it.

CHAPTER FIVE

LATE THE NEXT MORNING, Kit, a basket on her arm, strode down the narrow aisle at Branson's grocery as if she owned the place. She paused at a display of produce, taking dark satisfaction from the abrupt pause in conversation between Libby Fisk, former homecoming queen, and Heather Abernathy, former editor of the high school yearbook. It was probably Heather who'd written "Most likely to self-destruct by age twenty-one" in Kit's space in the yearbook.

Kit ignored them and focused with a studied nonchalance on the vegetables in front of her. Carrots held more interest than these two former members of the in-crowd.

Libby and Heather moved away, their conversation now a whisper.

Cursing under her breath, Kit tossed an onion into her basket. Why was she here? What had possessed her to cosign for her mother? Because Kit had always felt she was responsible for her mother, had always played the adult to Babe, the perpetual teenager. But what had it ever gotten her? Nothing. Worse than nothing. Babe had once lifted one of Kit's credit cards on a suspiciously chummy visit to Boston and had run up a whopper of a tab in mail-order lingerie before Kit had figured it out. Babe had laughed it off. Some mother.

Kit picked up a bell pepper and blew out a long exasperated breath. Spending the night on a warped floor under a kitchen table had made her exceptionally grumpy.

If her father had stuck around maybe their lives would have been different. Kit never knew him. Babe never talked about him. If they'd forged a real family, would Kit have ever heard the words *white trash?* For whatever reason, he hadn't stayed, and Kit had suffered the consequences.

She dropped a head of lettuce, a tomato and a pack of mushrooms into her basket, but couldn't get her negligent mother out of her mind.

A long, low wolf whistle followed her as she made her way through the produce section. She ignored it. Just as she'd ignored the scathing looks and hurtful gossip.

At one point in high school, she'd given up trying to convince everyone she wasn't Babe Jr. She'd begun acting out—except her specialty was never men. She preferred in-your-face anarchy.

It was only after moving to Boston, lying about her age and eking out a life separate from her mother's, that she had grown into her own. Of course, nobody in Pritchard's Neck would know about such a metamorphosis. They still saw her as the wild child of a wild child.

So be it. She was only in town until she could wipe Babe's slate clean and call it quits with her. And this dot on the map.

Kit moved halfway up the aisle to the tiny wine section. Although the utilities had been cut at Babe's house, Kit was determined to rough it there for the duration, even if it meant shopping at Branson's once a day. A grill and charcoal had been among the items destined for the yard sale, and she intended to buy a thick steak and the makings of a salad. She wanted a bottle of wine to toast the fact that, with this exorcism of Babe, she would finally break free of Pritchard's Neck.

"You want company drinking that, Kit-ten?" The taunting voice brought her up short.

She whirled around to confront Stu Hardy, a former football star and classmate, and possibly the most arrogant character in her high school experience. And now he was Babe's landlord. From the self-satisfied smirk on Hardy's face, he hadn't changed much. He placed both meaty hands on the shelving on either side of Kit's head, effectively pinning her in the aisle. He smelled of the same inexpensive cologne that lingered in Babe's house.

"Have you been following me?" Kit calculated the damage a boot heel could do to his unsuspecting instep.

"Perhaps." With a shrug he leaned in close. "Deep down, you and I were always two of a kind…."

PULLING HIS TRUCK into Branson's parking lot, Sean glanced at his watch. He only had a few minutes before his appointment with Candace. He'd called her to say he needed to get a few things clear. In person. After a morning of hauling traps, it was too bad he didn't have time to shower. Candace would just have to hold her breath. But he'd make time to pick up some antihistamine for Alex. With warmer weather and the windows wide open, her allergies had been acting up.

"Libby. Heather." He nodded to Alex's scout leaders deep in conversation just inside the store entrance. Both women dimpled at his greeting, and he headed to the over-the-counter medicine.

Unable to find any children's antihistamine, he made his way back to the front of the store for help. That's when Sean heard Libby and Heather, one aisle over, discussing his daughter.

At the sound of Alex's name, Sean stopped short.

"—that child needs a woman's touch," Libby was saying.

"I agree," Heather replied. "But Sean seems to think there's nothing wrong."

"There's nothing wrong if you want to raise a girl without femininity or social skills."

"What can you expect when she's been brought up by three stubborn men?"

"Ooh, don't I know how stubborn they all are," Libby huffed. "Haven't I tried to fix Sean up? I liked Jilian as much as the next person, but she's been dead six years."

"Poor Alexandra." Heather sighed. "If she'd just get her feet out of those ridiculous lobster boots."

"What she needs is a mother."

Sean parted the cereal boxes and looked directly through the shelves to the opposite aisle. "Heather and Libby, stop meddling. Alex and I don't need anything."

The two women had the sense to look thoroughly embarrassed before they scurried to the checkout.

Sean shook his head. What he and his daughter really needed was to get the town twits off their backs.

Now where was that stock boy?

Irritated, Sean turned a corner and glanced down the aisle to the wine section. There was Stu Hardy, his back to Sean, putting the moves on some woman. Sean couldn't see her face.

He'd played football with Stu all through high school, quarterback to Stu's wide receiver. Like him, Stu had stayed in town after graduation, worked hard and bought up enough properties to make a good living as a landlord, as well as managing the store. He had a credible reputation as a member of the chamber of commerce. Local folks respected a hard worker, a successful businessman who hadn't forgotten his roots. Sean played handball with him every Friday. Stu was okay. A guy's guy. But Sean had heard rumors he was sometimes overbearing with the ladies.

With one particular lady at the moment, if the scene in the wine section was to be believed. Sean caught a glimpse of red cowboy boots. Noticed the woman trying to extricate herself from Stu's advances. Noticed the woman was…Kit Darling, her face a mask of indignation. Not the most sensitive toward women, Stu probably considered Kit fair game based on her mother's reputation alone.

Well, not today. A sour feeling in the pit of his stomach, Sean saw a man pressuring a woman, and the father in him, a man raising a daughter, was outraged. He headed down the aisle toward Stu and Kit.

The former wide receiver was leaning in for the pass. "So, want to share that bottle?"

"Give it a rest, Stu." Sean clamped a hand on Stu's shoulder.

"Sean, my man!" Stu slapped Sean's shoulder as if they were tight friends. "I'm just asking Kitten, here, for a drink. Kind of a welcome-home gesture."

Cocking one eyebrow, Sean looked to Kit for confirmation.

A wine bottle clutched in her hands, she looked so small, like some bellicose pixie, fiercely standing her ground. And including him in the same spitfire gaze she leveled at Stu. Had he expected thanks for butting in?

"Am I interrupting?" Sean asked Kit pointedly.

"No," she said, ice just below the surface of her words. "This conversation was going nowhere."

"Sorry, Stu." Sean planted himself closer to Kit.

Stu shrugged, affecting indifference. "It was just a little cordial business." He gave Kit the quick once-over, then turned to Sean. "You do know I'm Babe's landlord."

He'd forgotten.

Kit narrowed her eyes. She might know, but she didn't like it.

"If you plan to stay in town for any length of time," Stu continued, winking slyly at Kit, "I thought you might want to keep the same payment 'arrangement' Babe and I had."

"You heard the lady, Stu." Sean bristled. "She's not interested." Rumor about Stu's womanizing was one thing, but this was an eye-opener.

"Hey, man, just kidding around." Stu hesitated, then leveled a scornful look at Sean. "McCabe, I thought you had better things to do than play Dudley Do-Right. Guess I had you pegged wrong." He turned and swaggered toward the front of the store.

"I usually fight my own battles," Kit said, her smoky eyes smoldering.

Man, this woman didn't give an inch. The surprise slap she'd administered in the hospital parking lot last night came painfully to mind. Obviously, she was still in striking mode.

"Don't take it personally," he replied, unable to keep the edge out of his voice. Why did she push his buttons? "I dislike bullying."

She stood before him, a go-to-hell attitude in her posture. Spiky hair capped a face to make angels weep. He dragged his gaze from her generous mouth etched in dark purple to the tiny gold hoops piercing her left eyebrow. She still had the power to rattle him. *Incendiary* described Kit Darling to a tee.

She waited and watched as if issuing a challenge, and he felt the allure of a walk on the wild side as strongly as he had a decade ago.

Hell, was he any better than Stu Hardy?

Kit grabbed a second bottle of wine off the shelf, then turned and stalked in the direction of the cashier, striking attitude in the flounce of her shoulders, the sway of her behind and with every staccato beat of those lethal cowboy boots.

What would it be like to walk away like that? To turn your back on this town and say to hell with it all. He thought of Alex and instantly knew. It would be empty. He could never trade the ordinary, predictable joys of fatherhood for a month of care-free Sundays.

Still, that didn't prevent him from groaning audibly when he saw Kit cross Branson's parking lot to straddle that monster of a Harley. She took off, without a helmet, her purple hair spiking in the wind.

"Wow!" The missing stock boy materialized at Sean's side. "She's something, huh?"

Yeah.

Sean had stopped in for antihistamine and had ended up with an undefined yearning in his gut that wouldn't quit. Worse, he was now late for that meeting with Candace.

KIT TOOK THE LONG WAY back to Babe's rental, down around the harbor. She stopped by the pier to watch the lobstermen refueling and changing out bait barrels. If she didn't hate this town so much, it would make a great backdrop for a Sea-faring Cecil episode: the unforgiving rocky coast-line, the men—and a few women—against the sea.

She paused, suddenly realizing she *had* paid

homage to this way of life. Here she thought she'd left her hometown and its people behind, while she'd actually glorified them in Seafaring Cecil. She'd made him a fisherman from a small town, looking for adventure. And she hadn't consciously realized it. Seems the old bromide was true: you could take the girl out of the small town, but you couldn't take the small town out of the girl. How rich!

She laughed aloud, startling a flock of gulls that had just settled on the punt wharf pylons. It seemed, despite her protests to the contrary, she was drawn to these rugged, small-town people who devoted their lives to such a capricious line of work.

Like Sean.

Yet again, she tried and failed to push him from her thoughts.

What made him feel he had to play the knight in shining armor? First he'd tried to help out after that dumb yard sale, then he had to catch her off guard by apologizing for his rude sister. And just now, what had possessed him to butt in with that Neanderthal Hardy? She certainly hoped she hadn't led Sean to believe she needed rescue. She could take care of herself.

Besides, he didn't seem to enjoy rescuing her. On the contrary, he seemed downright peeved about it. In high school, he'd been an outgoing kind of guy, but now he seemed gruff, closed. In some ways, solitary like herself. Except with Alex. With Alex, Sean was warm and the epitome of a good father. Kit always felt you could judge the worth of a man by how he treated animals and small children. And Sean treated his child with respect, as if he understood the individual she was.

An attractive concept, respect.

Taking a deep gulp of sea air, Kit eased her Harley onto the road. For the very reason she admired Sean, she wanted to avoid him. For that ability to look beneath the surface. For his love of family. Home and hearth. Those last weren't her thing.

Her ride back to Babe's took her past a brand-spanking-new sign advertising McCabe Lobster Pound, Opening July 1. An older and a younger man with dark good looks—surely Sean's father and a brother—worked on the almost completed facility. It appeared as if the McCabes had sunk a lot of time, effort and money into the project. Sean wasn't planning on leaving Pritchard's Neck anytime soon.

They came from two different worlds that barely intersected.

So why couldn't she get him out of her mind?

One reason was apparent a few minutes later as she turned into Babe's driveway. Alex. Sitting on the front porch steps, clutching a large shopping bag. Kit would bet her last dollar the bag contained Seafaring Cecil books just waiting to be autographed. Ah, hero worship—and from such a terrific kid—could prove dangerously heady.

"Kit!" Alex bounded off the steps as she brought the Harley to a halt. "You promised to autograph my books."

"So I did." Kit unloaded her small sack of groceries from the motorcycle's rear compartment. "But didn't you promise to stay with your uncle and grandfather?"

"I'm allowed to read when I finish my school assignments. And I finished." The swelling had gone down on the shiner, but half of Alex's face was several shades of yellowing purple. "I was reading on your porch."

All probably true, but none of it a real answer to Kit's question.

"Let me put these groceries in the cooler, then I'll autograph your books…then I'm walking you back to the lobster pound."

"I'll wait right here."

What harm could it do to autograph the kid's books before returning her to her family?

Alex waited patiently for her hero to come back out. She wanted two things, and now that the first one was in reach—Kit autographing her books— she wasn't about to mess up the second. She didn't want to scare Kit off by being too forward. She often was, according to her teacher; pushy, Nina and Olivia called it. She'd heard Aunt Mariah tell Dad that Kit was a wild thing, and Alex knew you had to be patient with wild things. If you wanted them to stick around, you mustn't scare them. Alex sure didn't want to scare Kit off. No, she wanted Kit to stick around and be her friend.

And she wanted a ride on that motorcycle.

She glanced down at her wrist. Oops! Better hide the watch or her plan wouldn't work. She stuffed the watch in her overalls just as Kit came back outside.

"Okay, kiddo, let's see what you have here." Kit sat next to her on the step.

"All your books!" Alex crowed.

"All my books. My, my."

Alex eyed the leather motorcycle jacket on the floor just inside the screen door. "Can I try on your jacket?"

"Okay." Kit seemed cool with it. She leaned to open the door, then dragged the jacket out. Alex put it around her shoulders.

It was big, but not way big. Kit was bigger than Alex, but lots smaller than Dad. The jacket smelled of leather and something else. Something not from Pritchard's Neck. "What's this neat smell?"

"Patchouli." Kit smiled. "It's an East Indian mint. It's my favorite incense."

"What's incense?"

"Something you burn to make a room smell good."

"Oh." Alex thought about that for a minute. "Then my favorite incense is the wood shavings Dad burns in the Franklin stove in the pound."

"I bet that would smell good." Kit got a funny dreamy look in her eyes, then she shook her head and sat up straight. "Okay. Down to business. Tell me a little bit about yourself so I can make these inscriptions more personal."

Oh, that was easy! Alex could tell Kit a lot if it would keep them here on the step, just the two of them.

"I like cookie-dough ice cream. I hate turnips. I want a dog. I wish I was bigger so I could go out lobstering as Dad's sternman. And my favorite color is red."

"Mine, too."

"I know. We could be related."

Kit chuckled. "Have you ever been outside Maine?"

"Nope. But I'd like to go on the Bluenose to Nova Scotia."

"Why Nova Scotia?"

"Cause Pop Pop comes from there. Cape Breton. Have you ever been there?"

"As a matter of fact, I have. I saw bald eagles nesting there."

"Cool!" Alex grinned. "I wish I could travel."

"I bet you will someday. And Nova Scotia would be a great place to start." Kit wrote something in one of the books. "Maybe your Dad will take you over on the ferry one day. You could research your ancestors."

"Ancestors was a vocabulary word this year." Alex snuggled into the depths of Kit's leather jacket. "Confidential was the biggest one on the list today. You know what that means?"

"Secret."

"I'll tell you a secret if you tell me one."

"I thought the whole point of secrets was not to tell."

"Well, you won't die if you tell."

The corner of Kit's mouth twitched. Kinda like a smile that she was trying to hide. "Okay. What's your secret?"

Alex hesitated. She hadn't even told Dad this one. "Sometimes…sometimes I like the girly stuff my cousins wear. Sometimes."

"Yeah? Like what?"

"Sometimes Aunt Emily buys them neat bracelets. But that's all!"

"Bracelets are fun." Kit didn't look all weirded-out by this secret. "All cultures adorn their bodies in some way. Paint. Shells. Feathers. Jewelry. Why should we be any different?"

Alex breathed a sigh of relief. "Now you. What's your secret?"

Kit took her time. Like she might have a bunch of secrets. "Back in Boston, I sleep with a teddy bear," she said at last. "His name is Aldo."

"You do?" Alex tried to be as cool as Kit had been with Alex's secret although she'd always thought sleeping with stuffed animals was for babies. "I guess that's kinda like me sleeping with my cat. Inkspot."

"Inkspot would like Egypt. Cats were once worshipped there—"

"Oh my gosh!" Alex put on her best surprised expression. Time to put part two of her plan in operation. "What time is it?"

Kit glanced at her watch. "Two o'clock. Why?"

"I'm supposed to be at the pound when Dad gets there. I'm late!"

"Come on." Kit plunked the book she held into the shopping bag. It looked like a cloud had crossed her face. "I'll walk you back to the pound and try to explain."

"That'll take too long!" Alex looked right at that big red motorcycle. "Can't you gimme a ride? Puhleeze?"

CHAPTER SIX

"I'M SORRY I'M LATE," Sean said as the school secretary ushered him into Candace's office. "I had to stop for antihistamine for Alex."

"Where is Alexandra?" Candace looked up from her desk as Sean entered. She appeared more professional and aloof than usual. "If she's having a problem with her assignments, she should be here."

"It's not about her assignments." Sean took the chair Candace motioned to. He suddenly felt ten again and in trouble in the principal's office. "I need to explain yesterday."

Candace lowered her eyes and straightened some already straight papers on her desk. "Ah, yesterday."

"I know it looked like a free-for-all—"

"It didn't look educational, that's for certain." Tenting her fingers in front of her, Candace looked every inch the administrator. "Tell me…is Ms. Darling the child care you found for Alexandra?"

It was a dance of sorts—Candace knew far more than she was acknowledging—and he had to pay the piper. "No. Emily was watching her, but she wandered off in search of books at a yard sale. Kit Darling's yard sale."

"In search of Ms. Darling's books?"

"You're aware she's a writer?"

Candace paused as if carefully considering her words. "You know I've taken a special interest in Alexandra. When her attachment to Seafaring Cecil started to get her into mischief, I looked up the online site. To see if it was age appropriate."

"You did?" Sean didn't know which surprised him more—that Candace knew of Kit's work or that she had admitted a special interest in Alex. "And do you think it is?"

"The site is wonderfully creative. Ms. Darling certainly knows how to draw the viewer in. I can see why Alexandra is fascinated with her." Candace colored slightly. "I can see why anyone would be fascinated with her."

In a very classy way, Candace had just given him the opening to let her know his intentions. She deserved the truth.

"Candace, I didn't even know Kit was back in town. I went to retrieve Alex, it started to rain. We were hurrying to get the yard sale stuff under cover when the two of us fell. I tried to block her fall. You happened along when things looked… compromising."

"Ah."

"I'm not involved with Kit…in a personal way."

"Things would never be dull with her." Candace's voice had lost its professional tone.

"No, they wouldn't," he admitted.

"Perhaps she would be worth a second date."

He felt decidedly uncomfortable. He'd never called Candace after their first. "Don't talk about worth, Candace. If any woman is worthy, you—"

"I'm out of line. I apologize." She straightened her shoulders and returned to professionalism, offering a tentative smile. "I may have an education degree, Sean, but I know my chemistry. It's either there or it isn't."

"It will be for both of us one day."

"Just not together."

"I'm afraid not."

"You know I will still take a special interest in Alexandra."

"There's no doubt in my mind."

"Well…who's watching Alexandra now that Emily's had her baby?"

"My father and brother when I'm on the water." He glanced at his watch. "Which reminds me I'd better check in. They must be wondering what's kept me." He reached for his cell phone, then remembered Kit still had it. "May I use your phone?"

"Of course." Pushing the phone across the desk,

she turned to a graph on her computer screen. Did his eyes deceive him, or did her fingers tremble?

Not completely at ease himself, Sean, nonetheless, punched in Pop's cell number.

"McCabe here."

"Pop, I'm running late. Can I speak to Alex?"

"Alex!" Pop bellowed into the echoing pound without lowering the phone. "Front and center!"

Sean wanted to ask if his daughter had done her school work, if she'd stayed out of trouble, but not in front of Candace. He didn't want to give her the impression that matters were anything but under control.

"Jonas!" Pop again, still shouting, still holding the receiver too close. "Have you seen Alex?"

Sean didn't like the sound of this. "Pop?"

"She finished her school work, then said she was going to read. I assumed she'd curl up in the office, but she's not there."

"I thought she was with you, Pop." Jonas's voice threaded through from the other end of the line. "She's not out on the wharf."

"Son—"

"I'll take care of it. Thanks, Pop." Trying to keep his voice even and his features noncommittal, Sean put down the receiver. If Alex wasn't at the pound, he knew exactly where he'd find her.

"Anything wrong?" Candace looked up from the computer.

"Not at all. I just need to get back." He paused at the door. "I want you to know I'm doing the best I can."

"I know you are. No one ever said parenthood was easy." Candace's expression became serious. "We all want what's best for Alexandra. Remember that when the panel meets to review her situation."

Her words followed him like an ominous cloud as he made his way to the parking lot, then toward Kit's. Would this panel keep a bright child back a grade just because she needed to learn to stick to the rules?

If there were ever people who understood bridling under imposed rules, they were Sean, his father and Jonas. That's why they'd decided to go into business together. So that they could make their own rules. Did that make the village gossips Libby and Heather right? Raised by the three of them, is that why Alex got into trouble? Did she need a woman's touch? If so, iconoclastic Kit wasn't the right woman.

What the—!

Ahead in the Darling driveway Kit sat on her Harley, ready to take off. And there, dangerously perched on the seat behind her, in an oversized leather jacket and a helmet that flopped back and forth on her head, was his daughter.

Damn!

Did Kit have one ounce of common sense?

He slammed on the brakes in front of the house,

nearly giving eighty-two-year-old Frederica Harp-swell, out walking her little dog, a coronary.

"Alex!" Sean bounded out of his truck. "Get off that machine right now!" he shouted at his daughter.

Obviously, Alex couldn't hear him above the roar of the engine, but she saw him and waved jubilantly.

Kit cut the motor.

"Are you crazy?" He glowered at Kit as he hoisted Alex from the motorcycle.

"It's not what you think—"

"You're lucky I don't bring you up on endangerment charges!"

"But—"

"I don't want to hear it."

"Dad—"

"I don't want to hear it from you, either, Alex." He undid the helmet she wore, took it off, then shoved it at Kit who sat openmouthed on that monster of a machine.

"Have you forgotten you're suspended from school? Have you forgotten you're supposed to stay with Pop Pop and Uncle Jonas?" he snapped. "You're not supposed to be riding around town on a motorcycle. At any time. Ever."

"But Dad—"

"Not another word." He pulled the leather jacket from her tiny shoulders. Shoved it at Kit. "There's a big difference between imagining you're riding a motorcycle and really riding one. It's high time you learned the difference between fantasy and reality. And you—" He glared at Kit. "You do not ride an eight-year-old on a motorcycle. Not my eight-year-old."

His heart racing with the awful possibilities, he marched Alex toward his truck.

"Why, you overbearing son of a—" Kit followed right behind him. "Do you ever listen? Alex has done nothing so wrong as to warrant being bundled off like some piece of baggage. Nothing, do you hear?"

He tried not to. Instead, he opened the driver's side door, then lifted Alex onto the bench seat. Wiping away tears, she scooted over and into her safety booster seat.

"You're frightening the child!" Kit protested.

Her grip on his arm would make a longshoreman proud. He turned around.

"She needs to be frightened," he snarled, parental protection—and, yes, fear—rising hot inside him. "So she doesn't do stupid and dangerous things like take a ride on a motorcycle with a stranger."

He clamped his mouth shut. Not in front of Alex.

"Ask your daughter what happened." Kit glared right back at him. As if he were somehow in the wrong. "Ask her."

"I don't need to." He swung himself behind the

wheel, then slammed the door. "I saw all I needed to see."

"You're myopic, McCabe. Just like all the other self-righteous citizens of this town. Open your eyes. Maybe Alex's acting out is partly your fault. Maybe you're not listening to her. Maybe you're smothering her. Maybe—"

He started the truck, then turned on the radio to tune Kit out. With a cursory glance in either direction, he pulled onto the road and headed for the pound. Every woman in town, from Libby and Heather to Emily and Candace, wanted to give him advice on raising his motherless daughter. He didn't need one more word.

Especially not from Kit.

What the hell did she know about parenting? About a proper family life? What could she tell him about helping his daughter fit in? She'd flaunted her nonconformity at every turn.

He slammed his fist on the steering wheel.

"Dad." Alex spoke quietly from the other side of the cab. "We weren't going for a ride."

"That's not what it looked like."

"We weren't going anywhere. And that's the truth."

"Then what in he—" He caught himself. "Then what were you doing on the back of that motorcycle?"

Even restrained in her safety seat, Alex sat up taller, crossing her arms over her thin chest. "I asked Kit to give me a ride home because I wanted to be at the pound when you got there. But she wouldn't."

He didn't interrupt. Didn't ask what Alex was doing with Kit in the first place. He tried to listen for the truth amid the storytelling.

"She said I could wear her jacket and her helmet and sit behind her in the driveway, then she was gonna walk me back to the pound. She said I wasn't old enough to really ride on the back of a motorcycle."

"She said that?"

"Scout's honor." Alex solemnly raised three fingers. His daughter was a spinner of tales, but she wasn't an out-and-out liar.

"So you just got to sit on the motorcycle."

"For one minute." She scowled. "Which you interrupted. So I have twenty-nine seconds left."

He shook his head ruefully. Hadn't he just gone to let Candace know she'd jumped to conclusions about what she'd seen in the wake of the yard sale? Hadn't he been angry at his family and most of the town for jumping to conclusions about Kit?

He blew out a long, low breath. "I'm sorry for flying off the handle, sweet pea." He reached across the seat for his daughter's hand, squeezed it gently. Felt a fool. "Forgive me?"

"Sure." Alex smiled. "You gonna apologize to Kit?"

That was the crunch. "Yeah. I will."

"When?"

"The next time I see her."

"When? She's not gonna be in town long."

"Soon."

"Right after you and Pop Pop and Uncle Jonas finish working on the pound today?"

"Then it'll be time for supper."

"After supper?"

His daughter could wear down a stone. But this time she was right. "Tonight," he agreed. "Right after supper."

If he felt the fool now, how would he feel standing in front of that spitfire of a woman?

KIT WAS LIVID. She kicked a clod of dirt.

"Oooohhhh!" She shook her fist after the retreating truck. "You insufferable, overbearing, smug, unheeding, self-righteous, misguided man!" she shouted.

"He is quite a handful."

Kit whirled around to see an elderly woman in a broad-brimmed straw hat and exquisite kimono holding a tiny black-and-white dog.

"I beg your pardon?"

"Sean McCabe," the woman said in a British accent, "is quite a handful. But you seem up to the task of handling him." She stepped forward, smiling, her hand outstretched. "I'm Frederica Harpswell. And this is my dear Bitsy."

"A papillon!" Her anger toward Sean faded before this charming woman and her little fluff of a dog.

"You know the breed?"

"Oh, yes. I believe many years ago only the imperial Chinese family were allowed to own these dogs. The women would carry them around in their sleeves."

Frederica laughed softly. "I'm impressed. Not many people know that."

"I'm a trivia buff. My head is crammed with no-account facts."

"Ooh, hush!" The woman covered her dog's ears. "Bitsy doesn't like being thought of as trivial, or, worse yet, no-account."

"None of us do," Kit replied grimly.

"Ah, the young man. Most headstrong. But what young man isn't? You wouldn't want him all wishy-washy, now, would you?"

"I don't want him at all."

Frederica looked surprised, but let the comment slide. "I don't believe I caught your name, dear."

If she hadn't, she was the only one in town.

"Kit. Kit Darling."

"What a lovely name. Strong, but romantic." There wasn't a tinge of irony or sarcasm in the woman's words. "Are you in town long?"

"No. I have business, but it won't keep me."

Frederica beamed. "Forgive an old woman for being nosy, but does that business involve the handsome Mr. McCabe?"

"No." Kit didn't know why she felt this woman deserved an answer. Perhaps it was the kindness she saw in her eyes. "Sean McCabe's daughter found out I'm her favorite travel writer, but…oh, it's a long story."

"I have plenty of time. Too much, it seems. The hazard of outliving friends and loved ones." Frederica's smile briefly dimmed before she perked up again. "But I digress. You said you were a travel writer?"

"I write as Seafaring Cecil."

"Books? Articles?" The elderly woman appeared genuinely interested.

"More than just books. I have a Web site and a catalog of unusual items I've collected in my travels."

"An entrepreneur! How delightful! I'm one myself!"

Kit looked at the woman. "Harpswell? Not *the* Harpswells of Harpswell & Harpswell Bath Emporium?"

"One and the same. Do you know my products?"

"Absolutely! Your company is one of the cottage-to-big-time businesses I've read about. Wanted to emulate. I know your whole story."

"Well, not the whole story dear. A woman should have some secrets."

Kit grinned. She liked Frederica Harpswell. Heck, she'd admired Frederica for a long time. An English war bride, she'd begged her captain-of-industry husband for seed money to start a little business of her own, making soaps and candles and custom toilet waters. For forty years she'd managed to maintain a loyal clientele of women her own age while luring younger and younger women with innovative lines—never straying from the bath products she knew best. Her shops were in every mall in the country.

"Are you vacationing in Pritchard's Neck, Ms. Harpswell?"

"I used to. I started summering here in the fifties, but now I live here. And it's Frederica."

"You live here? Why, you could live anywhere."

"But Pritchard's Neck isn't just anywhere. I grew up on the rocky coast of Cornwall. This little bit of Maine—my husband's birthplace—feels like home."

"It's my birthplace, too. But I'd rather be in Cornwall."

"Don't be so hard on your hometown." Frederica placed a gentle hand on Kit's arm. "I know something about being an outsider. First, an English war bride, then a 'summer person,' of all things. My husband may have been born here, but I will always be from away." Frederica rolled her eyes dramatically. "But once I realized that being an outsider is only a state of mind, I fit in quite well."

"You did?"

"Well, that and I donate boodles of money yearly to good local causes." Frederica's laugh sounded like tiny bells. "Seriously, dear, my attitude was the real breakthrough."

"I'm glad for you, but I'm not staying."

"No? It sounds as if you could do your job from anywhere. Why not Pritchard's Neck?"

"Why Pritchard's Neck?"

"For starters, Sean and his daughter."

"Ha! Sean and his family seem to think I'm unfit to darken their doorways, let alone associate with Alex. If I stay in town much longer, the locals will claim I caused Alex's suspension from school."

"And did you?"

Kit harrumphed. "No. Alex is quite clever enough to get in trouble all by herself. But now that she's out of school, she has plenty of time to seek me out, and that's a problem. Seems I'm not considered a proper role model."

"I don't know about the rest of the McCabes, but Sean…well, Sean is wrestling with his daughter's attraction to you because he's fighting his own. Quite unsuccessfully, I might add."

"His own attraction?" Kit squeaked. "To me?"

"Who else are we talking about, my dear?"

"Oh, no!" The thought was appalling. "Sean and I are oil and water, flint and…and…"

"May I remind you that opposites attract?" Frederica's smile had turned most Cheshire-cat-like. "And that makes for a most interesting relationship. My husband—may his soul rest in peace—and I were total opposites. But, our differences kept the spark alive."

"I have no interest in fostering a spark."

Frederica raised one eyebrow. "Be that as it may, I'd like to invite you and Alex to tea at my house. Tomorrow at four?"

"Me and Alex? What about her suspension? What about her principal? And what about her father?"

"You won't hear a peep out of Candace Simmons. I funded the school's computer lab. And Sean? Well, I'm an old lady. A very respectable old lady, I might add. I'm a most suitable chaperone for his daughter." Frederica winked. "Now, Alex might not think tea a very exciting prospect. Just tell her I'm a well-traveled old lady, and I'll let her play my Australian didgeridoo."

"You want me to tell her? Why not you?"

Frederica smiled. "Because you're her friend, dear. I only hope to be. And yours, as well."

"I don't mean to be rude, but why?"

"You're not rude, just forthright. I like that. Moreover, I like your spark. I like your energy and your creativity. Besides…" She sighed deeply. "When my husband died two years ago…well, seclusion is very lonely. I think it's time I came out."

"With a twenty-four-year-old pariah and an eight-year-old troublemaker?"

"You two are probably the most interesting women in Pritchard's Neck. Now, say you'll come to tea and bring Alex."

Call her crazy, but Kit could use a friend. "I'll come."

"And Alex?"

"I'll talk to Sean." The man she never wanted to speak to again.

Frederica's smile lit her face. "Good girl!"

No one had ever called her that before.

THE SUN WAS SETTING when Sean finally made it to Babe's place, but there was enough light to see Stu's BMW in front and Kit's Harley parked at the side of the house. Landlord or not, why the hell couldn't this guy leave Kit alone?

And why did Sean feel so protective?

As he slid out of his truck and saw Kit and Stu

arguing on the front porch, he prepared for confrontation.

"What seems to be the problem?" he asked, heading across the bedraggled front yard, knowing full well he was stepping over the line. In public. Again.

Stu glared at him. "Kitten, here, seems to think she'll be getting a rental deposit back." He jutted a thumb in the direction of the broken porch railing, the one Sean had plowed through when he fell earlier. "With this damage? I don't think so."

"It's not the end of the month," Kit retorted, bristling. "By the end of the month, I'll have everything in order, including the railing."

"And how do you plan to do that?" Stu smirked as if he'd just caught her in a trap. "I know for a fact Babe didn't keep any tools around. I can't see you carrying any on that Harley. And rumor has it you don't have the spare cash to hire anyone."

"I'm doing the repairs." Sean stepped onto the porch next to Kit. Across from his old football buddy. On the opposite team now. "I broke the railing, and I'm fixing it."

"You are?" Kit and Hardy responded together. Sean couldn't figure out who looked more dumbfounded.

"Yeah. Got my tools in the truck." He did. He didn't have to say he had them from working on the pound.

"There's no juice." Hardy narrowed his eyes. "Electricity's shut off."

"Who needs electricity?" Unaccountably, Sean found himself digging in deeper. "Most of the houses in this town were built before power tools." He looked at Kit as if this had all been prearranged, then back at Stu. "So, now you know everything's taken care of, I guess you'll be shoving off."

Stu resisted. "I'll be back."

"I'm sure Kit will let you know when you can come for the final inspection. Until then, she has all the help she needs."

Stu cast him a disbelieving glance. "Yours."

"Mine." What had he gotten himself into?

"McCabe—" Stu Hardy shook his head "—I never figured you'd let go of Jilian's memory. Not for the likes of Kitten, here, that's for sure."

With a menacing look at Kit, he stepped off the porch and headed for the car.

Sean's first instinct was to go after him, to wipe the smirk off his face, but he felt a small firm hand on his arm, restraining him.

Kit had been unusually quiet.

He turned to her. "You okay?"

She nodded, but she seemed to be struggling with her emotions. Withdrawing her hand, she met his gaze. "What brings you here?"

"You're welcome."

"I…I didn't ask for your help. Didn't…don't need it," she replied stiffly.

"Relax. I did break the railing. And I'm going to fix it."

Every muscle in her compact and shapely body seemed tense and poised for fight. Or flight. "What do you expect to gain by helping me?"

He felt the muscles twitch along his jaw. "Not every male has ulterior motives."

"Ha!" She cocked her head and looked up at him, challenge flashing in her eyes. In the half-light of dusk, her feistiness was as appealing now as her vulnerability had been earlier. "Are you telling me you're the last vestige of shining knighthood?"

"I'm telling you I'm going to fix your railing."

"I can't pay you. Not even for the supplies."

"I broke the damn thing. I'm repaying you."

"Nothing's free. There are always strings attached. Always."

"I'm not Stu, Kit." Without thinking, he took her hand. It was small in his. Almost as fragile as Alex's but with calluses on the palm. The calluses melted his heart. "I'm just trying to do what's right."

"And is that really why you showed up just now?"

He felt heat rise up the back of his neck. "Sort of."

Abruptly, she pulled her hand from his. "What do you want?"

"Has anyone ever told you you're a difficult

woman?" Sean shook his head in exasperation, but couldn't suppress a grin. "You make it impossible to apologize."

"Apologize?" Kit's eyes grew wide in surprise.

"Yeah," he said. "Believe it or not, I was on my way over to apologize for this afternoon. About the motorcycle and all. Alex explained how you wouldn't take her for a ride. I jumped to the wrong conclusion. I'm sorry."

"You are?"

"Is it so hard to believe an overbearing, myopic, son of a something or other—I didn't quite catch it all—can apologize?"

She blushed, really blushed, to the roots of her streaked and spiky hair, and he discovered he liked being able to make her blush. But he wasn't as comfortable with the physical longing she made him feel.

"So…" He extended his hand, trying to get a grip on his libido with a cool and friendly handshake. "Truce?"

"Truce." She shook his hand, but didn't quite look him in the eye. After all the times she'd unnerved him, perhaps he had the power to unnerve her just a little. He felt that physical jolt again.

"But that leaves the question of the railing," she mused, quickly breaking the awkward moment. "How am I going to pay you? For the supplies, at least. I insist."

What was so difficult about accepting help? Or was it his help?

"I know." A smile lit her face. "I almost forgot. I can give your dad and brother a break for a couple hours tomorrow."

"I don't get it."

Her smile got wider. More sensuous. "Alex and I have been invited to tea. At Frederica Harpswell's."

"You have?" Now that was a shocker. Frederica Harpswell was as close as Pritchard's Neck got to royalty.

"Sure." Kit waved her hand dismissively. "Frederica and I go back…a long way. Anyway, she suggested I bring Alex. And if I did, Alex wouldn't be trying to sneak away to see me. You could even use the tea party as a good-behavior carrot."

"Tea?" He couldn't imagine who would be more out of place amid the crumpets. Kit or Alex.

"Why not?" There was an edge of mischief in Kit's voice. "Frederica is a proper role model for Alex, isn't she?"

"Sure. The best." Bemused, Sean shook his head. Emily would be green with envy. She'd never been invited to tea with Frederica Harpswell.

"Your family won't have a problem with Alex and me?"

"They shouldn't. As much as my family might want it otherwise, I don't run my life by committee. Besides, I'll make them understand."

"Understand what?" Kit appeared as uncertain as he of the next step. "What exactly is there to understand, Sean?"

That he'd stepped outside the pale of family and community expectations for Kit. Just how much of his mind had he lost to her? And the simple hot shower he'd planned on taking later? Even that had been complicated by the woman. He was going to have to take a cold one now.

CHAPTER SEVEN

"WHAT EXACTLY IS THERE to understand?" Kit repeated, not sure she wanted an answer.

After a very long pause, he said, "That we've worked something out in Alex's best interest."

Ah, Alex. Okay, that was fairly safe. Except for the *we* part. Kit didn't want to roam into the realm of we with Sean.

"So," she said, "Alex can come to Frederica's for tea."

"Yeah." He looked as wary as she felt. "What time?"

Kit didn't know if she was pleased or not.

"Four o'clock," she replied.

"I'll drop Alex off at Mrs. Harpswell's, then pick her up...when? How long does tea last?"

Suddenly, he looked out of his league. A rugged outdoorsman undone by tea. Kit grinned and let down her own guard. "How should I know? This is a first for me, too."

"Hey, you're the world traveler. You should have picked up a tea party or two along the way."

"The Queen of England asked me once, but I was on-site with Bob Ballard."

"The guy who found the *Titanic?*"

"Yeah."

"You're kidding."

"About the queen, yes. So, since my tea party experience is nonexistent, why don't I walk Alex home when we're finished. That way you won't have to leave work on the pound twice."

"You know about the pound?"

"Alex told me."

They lapsed into awkward silence.

"She likes you." Sean cleared his throat as if it pained him to admit as much. "Alex likes you."

"I like her."

"I mean she really likes you. Admires you." He scowled. "Which brings up the whole motorcycle business."

Kit bristled. "I told her she was too young to ride."

"I'm not talking about her on the bike." He skewered her with a dark gaze, and she realized she could get lost in those brooding eyes. "I'm talking about you on the bike. As a role model."

How dare he? "Cecil is a role model. I didn't ask to be—"

"That's not how it works with kids. Sometimes

you don't get to choose. You get chosen. And when you get chosen by an eight-year-old—my eight-year-old—you get responsibilities."

"What are you talking about?" Kit drew herself up as tall as she could, but she still only came to Sean's shoulder. "I ride responsibly."

"You ride without a helmet." His words were matter-of-fact. His eyes, however, burned a hole in her staunch love of freedom.

She chose her words with care. "Last I knew, Maine was one of the states without a helmet law."

"I know all the freedom-of-choice arguments. And I know all the safety issues. I don't want to debate you on this. As a parent, I'm asking you to set an example for a little girl who thinks the world of you."

"As a Seafaring Cecil fan, she's seen me do far more dangerous things than ride a motorcycle without a helmet."

"I'm having some difficulty getting her to make the distinction between reality and fiction." He knit his brows as if this admission were a painful act of going public. "Seafaring Cecil is your career persona. A kind of stuntperson. I can make her see that. But Kit Darling is who you are. Flesh and blood."

Kit flinched. Could he possibly know that Seafaring Cecil helped her escape Kit Darling?

"As to the flesh and blood, when you ride that bike, I expect to see less blood and more—" He stopped abruptly, a lock of dark hair falling rakishly over his forehead, color rising beneath his tan. "That didn't come out the way I meant."

"Really." Kit suppressed a grin.

"Besides…" He recovered his composure, stared hard at her. "There are people who care about you."

"Sure." She looked away from his intense gaze. Looked across the street, between the houses to the mouth of the harbor where the lighthouse beam speared the distant and darkening horizon with an unrelenting rhythm. As popular as Seafaring Cecil had become, Kit remained alone. "Cecil fans."

"I'm not talking about Seafaring Cecil." With work-roughened fingers, he gently turned her chin so that she looked at him. "I'm talking about Kit," he said, his voice ragged.

"I'll wear a helmet when I'm in town," she said quickly. Too quickly. She capitulated where she would normally stand her ground because she needed him to remove his fingers from her face. She was frozen by his touch and his concern. "For Alex."

"You will?"

"Yeah." *Now, please, let me go.*

"One more thing." He spread the long fingers of his large hand along the side of her face, lowered his face closer to hers. "I think we need to get this out of the way."

He cupped her face in both hands and lowered his mouth to kiss her.

His lips were warm and firm against hers, his touch surprisingly insistent. She shivered as he traced her lower lip with his tongue. He smelled like sawdust and the sea. Home and away. She swayed a little from the heady mix.

Even as his fingers combed through her hair, he pulled away with a soft growl. Cool evening air rushed between them.

"What was that all about?" she asked, struggling to clear her head.

"I never got a first-date kiss." He grinned, obviously pleased with himself. "Might never have gotten one. You used to say kissing was outdated bourgeois romanticism. But from that first time we started working on the geography project back in high school, I wanted a kiss." His grin melted into one long sexy look. "For starters."

Kit swallowed. Hard. As if that would slow her racing pulse.

His expression turned from sexy to dead serious. "That out of the way, maybe now we can be friends. For Alex."

"That kiss was for Alex?"

"No. That kiss was to clear the air. Between us."

"And it certainly did," she lied on a sharp exhalation.

She could still feel his lips on hers. His breath on her cheek. His hands in her hair.

"So…I'll bring Alex by Mrs. Harpswell's at four tomorrow." Standing in the light of the rising moon, he seemed suddenly detached, unaffected by the kiss. Cool. Like the big man on campus he once had been. "Then I'll fix your railing tomorrow evening," he continued, "and we can call it even."

"Even. Sure." She had never felt more unsure and uneven in her life. All because of Sean's touch. His kiss.

Get a grip. He just wanted to settle things and move on. For Alex.

He turned, and, as she watched him go, she wondered if he could possibly imagine the unsettling inequality between them. He was so experienced. To him, a kiss could simply be a means to clear the air and move on. She hadn't yet learned the sliding scale of kisses. That not every kiss meant attraction.

She'd substituted travel for sex. If anyone in Pritchard's Neck knew how sexually inexperienced Kit Darling truly was, they'd get their laugh for the week.

"See you tomorrow," Sean called from the roadside.

"Sure," she whispered. A part of her dreaded the thought. Another part couldn't wait.

He waved casually as he pulled away in his truck, and she sat on the top step, determined not to moon over either him or that kiss.

Her arm rested on a box left over from the yard sale. She needed to get rid of this junk. Tomorrow. Before the tea. She suddenly thought of the scrapbook Alex had found. The one Babe must have kept of Kit's successes as Cecil. It was so typical of Babe to have kept the book secretly instead of praising her.

Kit scrambled to her feet. She'd find the scrapbook and give it to Alex. It would mean more to her as a present from Seafaring Cecil than it would to Kit as a reminder of her mother's misplaced attentions.

In the moonlight she could see the plastic laundry basket with the scrapbook, perched on a pile of pillows. Lifting the scrapbook out, Kit noticed at the bottom of the basket a short stack of envelopes, maybe a dozen or more, wound with a rubber band.

She retrieved her flashlight from inside the front door.

The return address on the top envelope read, in a feathery script, *Sr. Angelica, Convent of the Sacred Heart, York, Maine.* The address: *Ms. Cynthia Darling, 178 Larkspur Lane, Burlington, Vermont.*

Burlington had been Babe's hometown until she'd moved to Pritchard's Neck at eighteen. Single and pregnant with Kit.

Why had a nun written to Babe, who never professed an interest in religion, organized or otherwise?

Setting the scrapbook down, Kit lifted the envelopes from the basket, removed the rubber band and scanned the return addresses. They were all from Sister Angelica. The postmarks were all in December, the letters stacked in chronological order, each a year apart.

Kit glanced at the postmark on the top envelope and did some quick math. Babe would have been fifteen that year. Kit opened the envelope and pulled out a Christmas card. Inside was a mass card with a personal note below the printed greeting: *Cynthia, know that your personal trials have enriched the lives of others. Love yourself. God loves you. Sincerely, Sr. Angelica.*

Kit didn't understand.

She opened the next envelope, postmarked a year later. Another Christmas card. Another mass card. This time Sister Angelica had written, *I will do what I can to honor your request, but you must move on with your life. We all make mistakes, but God's love and forgiveness are infinite. I will pray for you in the new year.*

As Kit tore open the third envelope, the mass card fluttered to the floor. *Patience, Cynthia. God answers our prayers in unexpected ways.*

The fourth Christmas card held a photo of a little girl with blond curls standing on a chair, dressed in party finery and wearing a silly paper hat. She was blowing out three candles on a cake. At the edges of the photo stood a man and a woman, visible in the picture only as disembodied arms supporting the child on each side. Nothing was written on the back of the photo.

Inside the card Sister Angelica had written, *Rest assured she is loved and growing like a weed in the fresh sea air. Go in peace.*

Kit tore open the other cards. More mass cards. More calming assurances of God's love, but no more mention of the photo or of the child. The last envelope was postmarked fifteen years ago.

Why had a nun felt the need to offer Babe yearly assurances? And who was the little girl? A sinking feeling in the pit of her stomach told Kit she could figure out the answer if she dared put her mind to it. Did she have an older sister? Had Babe moved from Vermont to "the fresh sea air" of Pritchard's Neck to find her daughter? Had she found her? Here? Right now, only Babe knew, and Babe was missing.

Tomorrow Kit would call the Convent of the Sacred Heart in York. If she had a sister, she wanted to know.

Unfortunately, finding out would mean more, not less, involvement in Babe's life. In Pritchard's Neck.

She truly believed she could handle anything that surfaced from her mother's checkered past. She did not, however, think she could handle much more exposure to Sean.

Not after that kiss.

"DON'T YOU THINK Sunday's too soon for a family get-together?" Holding her new nephew, Mariah perched at the foot of Emily's hospital bed. "You're going home tomorrow. Probably not till afternoon. That only leaves Friday and Saturday to rest up for the onslaught."

"Do you actually think I'm going to rest any time in the next twenty years?" Emily smiled. She wasn't complaining. In fact, she was in her element. She was a wife and mother and queen of her own personal domain. She loved it. And she loved entertaining.

"Besides," she added, "Nick and Chessie and the girls will be in town to close on their house and register the girls for school next fall. A family party will be fun. Maybe I'll have it catered." Emily was feeling alive and downright sunny. No postpartum blues for her.

"Catered?" Mariah raised an eyebrow. Emily loved her sister-in-law, but her Yankee frugality sometimes made her unimaginative. "I know Brad just got a raise, but—"

"Oh, I don't mean anything elaborate. Just something simple from the Cove. Millicent could use the business…and the distraction. How's she holding up? Has she heard anything from Ed?"

"Nothing. Still AWOL with Babe Darling."

"That woman." Emily reached for her son, then held him in a protective embrace. "It would be better for everyone if she never showed her face in town again. Better if her daughter left town, too."

Mariah frowned. "I'm afraid there are two people who would disagree."

"Alex, sure…but you can't mean Sean." Emily thought she'd gotten through to her brother-in-law.

"I don't know. Tongues are wagging," Mariah continued. "Seems Stu Hardy was hitting on Kit in Branson's this morning, and Sean stepped in."

"Oh, I can't believe Kit Darling would find Stu's advances unwelcome." Now there was a match made in heaven.

Mariah shrugged. "I wasn't there. I only know my little brother has a real knight-in-shining-armor streak. And six years alone…well, he's vulnerable."

"To Kit? Oh, for heaven's sake! She's not his type."

"He found her attractive in high school, and she was even more outrageous then."

"This won't do," Emily said stiffly. She thought long and hard. "I'll call my cousin in Portland. She's about Sean's age. Single. A successful stockbroker. I'll invite her to the party Sunday."

Mariah shook her head doubtfully. "I can't see Sean with a stockbroker."

"Well, I can't see him with Kit Darling."

"Take it easy, Em. We're not talking wedding bells here." Mariah stroked little Eric's downy head. "Besides, you know Sean. Push him one way, and he'll deliberately go the other. The less we say or do, the better."

"I'm not so sure about that." Shivering, Emily pulled her son close. It was Babe that made her truly uneasy. Such a wasted life. And the thought of being related—in any way—to Babe was unacceptable.

"Sean's got his hands full with Alex and work," Mariah added. "I really don't think he has time for Kit. But if it will make you feel more comfortable, call your cousin."

"I will." Emily settled back into the pillows and nuzzled Eric. Identity was important. She'd learned that as a little girl. As a Chesterton. Now that she was a McCabe, it was her duty to preserve and strengthen that family identity. And there was no room for Darlings. Mother or daughter.

HOPING THE GRIN ON HIS FACE wouldn't arouse suspicion, Sean closed the kitchen door to the big house on the corner of Pier Road and Fisher's Lane, the rambling homestead he shared with Alex, Pop and Jonas. "I'm home!"

Over the television in the living room, two male voices grunted acknowledgment.

"Yippee!" Already dressed in pj's, Alex flew at him from the narrow back staircase. Climbing him like a capuchin monkey, she planted a big wet kiss on his nose. "Did you apologize to Kit?"

"Uh-huh." He had his little girl in his arms. It was safe to grin now. As much as he wanted. And, hot damn, he felt like grinning. "Now it's time for bed, squirt."

"Did she accept your apology?"

"Uh-huh." And the kiss, too. Surprisingly, Kit had accepted that kiss as if she'd wanted it as much as he had. Who'd have thought? "Bed."

"Can we see her again? Can we help her find a junk man? Can we invite her for a picnic on the islands?"

"Can you get into bed?" With a laugh, he peeled Alex's arms from around his neck. He swooped her high above his head, then brought her down to rub his chin whiskers against her neck. "Can you? Huh? Huh? Huh?"

"Ooooh, your beard!" Alex shrieked with delight. "You're gonna hafta shave before you take Kit out."

Take Kit out?

Right.

But why not?

Really.

He thought about the kiss. Thought about Kit's soft skin. About how, had he known the turn of events tonight, he could have—should have—shaved.

But it wasn't that kind of a kiss. It was a clear-the-air kiss.

It wasn't a leading-up-to-a-date kiss.

Dates were for people who had the slightest chance of a future together. Kit and he did not.

Too bad. Hell, he could admit his disappointment to himself.

"I just apologized, Miss Nosy McCabe," he replied, trying to act stern, but grinning instead. The thought of that kiss wouldn't go away. "I didn't ask for a date."

Alex tweaked his nose. "You should have."

"Hey, you're too young to know anything about dates."

"Am not!"

"Are too. And you're definitely too young to be up this late. Into bed." He plunked her solidly on the floor. "If you don't scoot right now, I won't tell you about your invitation. From Kit."

"An invitation?" She danced around him. "To what? To what? To what?"

"Have you had your bath?"

"And shampooed my hair."

"Brushed your teeth?"

She gave him a toothy grin. The toothpaste at the corners of her mouth reinforced the affirmative. "So what invitation?"

"First, upstairs. Into bed. Pull the covers under your chin. In ten...nine...eight..."

With a yelp of glee, Alex disappeared up the back stairs. He followed, the sound of his daughter's thumps and bumps gladdening his heart as he entered her bedroom. With one eye open, she lay absolutely still under her comforter of seagulls and lighthouses. He knew the suspense was killing her.

"Okay, punkin." He didn't have the heart to tease her any longer. "Kit would like you to come to tea with her at Mrs. Harpswell's house tomorrow afternoon."

"Tea?" His daughter suddenly looked crestfallen. "Are you sure Kit said tea?"

"She sure did."

"What happens at tea?"

"Beats me, kiddo, but Kit seemed pretty excited."

"Who's Mrs. Harpswell?"

"A friend of Kit's." He still puzzled over that relationship. "She lives on Pier Island. At the very end. The house with the great big telescope on the porch facing the lighthouse. I've heard she and her husband traveled all over the world. I bet she has terrific souvenirs and some stories that would make even Seafaring Cecil sit up and take notice."

"Maybe she's an adventurer, too." Interest returned to Alex's eyes. "Kit wouldn't have boring friends, would she, Dad?"

"Not if you and I are any indication."

"We are her friends, aren't we?" His daughter never missed an opportunity to make a point.

"I guess we are," he admitted. Friendship. Sealed with a kiss.

"Are you coming to tea?"

"Sorry. It's for female adventurers only." Although he wouldn't mind being a fly on the wall. "You're going to have to be on your best behavior," he warned with a mock scowl.

"Will do, Dad!"

He leaned down and kissed the top of her head, her hair still damp. "I love you, Alexandra Melinda McCabe."

"I love you, too." Yellow-green bruise around her eye and all, his daughter was a beauty.

"Time for prayers," he said, his voice catching.

Alex clasped her hands together on top of the comforter. "Now I lay me down to sleep. I pray the Lord my soul to keep. Guide me safely through the night, and wake me with the morning light. God bless—"

Sean prepared himself for the long litany of

family, friends, acquaintances and pets Alex usually lined up for blessings.

"God bless all the McCabes who ever lived," she continued quickly, "and, please, convince Kit to stay right here in Pritchard's Neck. Forever and ever. Amen."

Now, that had come out of the blue. Or had it?

From the moment Alex had met Kit, she'd wanted to make friends. Had made friends. From the start of that unusual friendship, Alex had wanted everyone she loved to like Kit, too. Had wanted to make a place in her life for a woman who claimed no place as her own.

He should remind Alex that Kit would be moving on. But he wouldn't disturb her happiness tonight. Not now. Not for twenty-four hours, at least.

"Night, sweet pea." He kissed her again.

"Night," she murmured, already drifting off.

He left the door ajar as he went out. In the hallway, he leaned against the wall. How should he handle the disappointment he knew was heading Alex's way?

In front of his daughter, in front of his family, in front of an old football buddy, even, he'd tried to make it seem as if Kit Darling's arrival in town was no big deal. But here he was, alone in the dark, with no one looking over his shoulder.

Could he admit that his fascination with Kit

hadn't faded one bit over the years? That that kiss hadn't cleared the air? It had only made him want her even more than before. As if that were possible.

CHAPTER EIGHT

KIT DID NOT NEED a tea party. She didn't need girl bonding with Frederica or Alex. She didn't need anything but to get out of Pritchard's Neck and back to work.

Irritation made her antsy and disagreeable after an unsuccessful morning. The junk man had wanted her to pay him to cart away Babe's things. She'd refused, although the only person Kit knew who had a truck for a haul to the dump was Sean, and she didn't see herself asking him for another favor. Then the consumer credit help agency she'd called from a pay phone had put her on hold for so long she'd been disconnected. When she'd tried repeatedly to redial, she'd been met by a busy signal. And finally, when she'd phoned the convent in York, the receptionist had told her Sister Angelica had died fifteen years ago—when the nuns used to run a home for unwed mothers. Informing Kit that all records were sealed for privacy, the woman had primly refused to discuss Cynthia Darling.

The only other people who might be able to en-
lighten Kit on Babe's relationship to the little girl in
the photo were Babe's parents. But Babe had broken with them by the time she was eighteen. Kit had
never met her Vermont grandparents and didn't
know if they were still alive. If they were, would
they want to reopen the past? Did Kit really want to?

She didn't know. And the not knowing com-
pounded her irritability. Her mood was as gloomy
as the day was sunny. Screw sunshine.

No, she didn't need, of all things, a tea party.

So why was she sitting on her Harley at the entrance to Frederica's grand harborside property?
Perhaps because Frederica's smile and Alex's unconditional acceptance were the only bright
spots—the only safe bright spots—in her personal
life at the moment.

She put the motorcycle in gear and slowly cruised
up the crushed-stone-and-shell drive. There was a lot
to see—a fabulous view of the harbor and the lighthouse, the gardens luxuriant in early June bloom, the
magnificent white house with its widow's walk at the
peak and its wide, all-encompassing veranda at the
base…. So why did her attention fix on the dinged
and dirty pickup truck parked out front? Sean's truck.

She had hoped he'd come and go before she arrived, leaving Alex and the prospect of nothing
more complicated than tea. Reluctantly, Kit parked

the Harley next to the truck, then climbed the steps and followed the voices around the veranda to the shady side of the house.

Frederica, looking every inch the queen, wearing an enormous beflowered hat and a gauzy ankle-length caftan, sat in a wicker fan chair. Her papillon sat, equally regally, on her lap. Alex, dressed in clean T-shirt, jeans and her lobstering boots, stood on a stool, gazing out to sea through an antique brass telescope. Sean, in a T-shirt that hugged his wide chest and jeans that accented his long legs, leaned against a pillar and watched her arrival.

"You're here!" Alex jumped from the stool, then bounded across the veranda to throw herself at Kit. "Mrs. Harpswell has the coolest stuff! Come look through the telescope."

"Just a minute, kiddo." Turning to Frederica, Kit held wide her arms, exposing her tank top, hiking shorts and high-top sneaks. "Hi. I'm sorry I didn't pack for tea."

"That's perfectly all right, my dear. I prefer to think of tea as a civilized state of mind. The important thing is, as Alex has so exuberantly put it, you're here." Her eyes sparkled and she seemed genuine in her welcome. "Besides, if we three decide to make it high tea, I have an attic full of vintage clothing."

"Any safari stuff?" Alex asked.

"I believe I still have the safari outfit my husband wore as a boy. Complete with pith helmet. It might just fit you."

"Cool!" With a grin that wouldn't quit, the eight-year-old hopped back on the stool to peer through the telescope again.

Kit was glad to hear the *we three* in the invitation to dress up. For a minute she'd feared Sean was staying.

"I'd better shove off," he said as if reading her thoughts.

"But what about your sternman dilemma?" Frederica turned from Sean to Kit. "Before you arrived, we were discussing the difficulties of lobstering. Mr. McCabe's sternman—"

"Please, call me Sean," he said.

"Then you must call me Frederica. It seems Mr. Mc—Sean's sternman has a family emergency, and his usual substitute has just had his heart broken and has gone off to Portland on what Sean describes as a bender."

And that makes it my problem, how? Kit wondered. But she also knew it was dangerous for a lobsterman to go out solo and perhaps more dangerous financially for him to lose a day fishing.

"I'm sorry, Frederica." Sean frowned. "I didn't mean to make you think you had to solve my problem."

"I didn't take it that way," she replied. "It's just that two, now three heads—" she gestured to Kit "—are better than one."

"I'll work something out," he replied. "I always do. It's just that school's still in session. In the summer I can usually snag one of the teenagers, looking for a few bucks."

"I have an idea." The sparkle in Frederica's eyes now suffused her entire expression. "You need a sternman, and our Kit is always on the lookout for a new travel story—"

"Wait a minute!" Sean and Kit chorused, stepping farther apart as if someone had thrown a poisonous snake between them.

"That's a great idea, Frederica!" Alex crowed. "Boy, oh, boy, I'd love to see my dad on Seafaring Cecil's Web site!"

"Oh, no!" Kit crossed her arms. "I'm here to clean up Babe's business, not start any of my own."

Alex looked thoroughly disappointed. "But you've only ever just mentioned lobstering. You never did a whole story on it. And it's really, truly cool!"

"I know, but—"

"I believe sternmen get twenty percent of the day's take," Frederica interjected, her look becoming more mischievous by the minute.

"It's not about the money."

"Then what is it?" Alex came across the veranda to stand right in front of Kit. "Dad helped you when you needed your stuff out of the rain."

Kit lay a hand gently on Alex's shoulder. "I believe you asked him to help me."

"Well, I'm asking you to help him now."

"Alex." Sean knelt beside his daughter. "Think about Kit for a minute. She's a little bit of a thing. Being a sternman, even for a day, is a tough job."

"Hold on there." Kit pulled herself up to her full five feet two inches. She didn't mind Sean thinking she didn't want to do the job, but she sure as heck didn't want him to think she couldn't do it. "Size has nothing to do with it."

As Frederica smiled benignly from the sidelines, Sean rose to stand before Kit. "Look, I know you've done a lot of rigorous—even dangerous—things, but being the sternman on a lobster boat is bull work. I've got four hundred traps. We pull most of them each day. From sunup till however long it takes. Usually mid-afternoon. No insult, but I don't think it's a job for you."

"I think you underestimate me, Sean."

"Kit…" His expression softened. "I have never once underestimated you."

"Then you have a substitute sternman for tomorrow," she replied, tilting her chin in defiance.

"I could use the money, and I certainly can handle the job. I won't take no for an answer."

"Sean, I believe we've solved your dilemma," Frederica declared.

Sean cocked his head in apparent disbelief. "I guess I'll see you at dawn. On the wharf behind my pound."

"I know where it is," Kit replied quickly before she was tempted to renege on the deal.

"I'll provide lunch and sunscreen," he said to her, before turning to Frederica. "Thank you." Then to Alex. "I love you. Be sweet."

He said nothing more to Kit, but sent her one long hungry look, leaving her momentarily woozy from the unexpected want in his eyes.

Peripherally, she saw Alex high-five Frederica, and suspected she'd been had.

So be it. Kit lived by a never-let-them-see-you-sweat code that had gotten her through dicier spots than a few hours on the water with Sean. Hard physical labor? So much the better. It meant she wouldn't have time or energy to be distracted by Sean's piercing dark eyes or that sexy if infrequent crooked grin.

Alex scampered along the edge of the veranda in a quick little victory dance. Lobstering wasn't exactly a date, but it was a step in the right direction. And who would have thought this Frederica could be so helpful? It was almost as if she wanted

Kit and Dad together, too. Alex said a silent thank you and a further I'm sorry for ever thinking tea might be boring.

Frederica rose from her chair, and her little black-and-white dog ran to dance around Alex's feet. "Ladies," she said, "if Sean will excuse us, I've had Karen set out tea in the library."

"You have your own library?" That was the ultimate luxury.

"And a rolling ladder," Frederica replied with a wink. "So that you can climb to the tippy-top shelves."

"This I gotta see!" Alex seized both Kit's and Frederica's hands. "See ya later, Dad!"

Kit held back a little. She was still looking at Dad. In a funny way. And Dad was still looking at Kit as if he might be wanting to undo the whole sternman deal.

No way was Alex going to let that happen. "Come on! I'm starving!"

"Alex, watch your manners," her dad warned.

"Okay," Alex agreed even as she gave a determined tug, urging Kit and Frederica into the house.

"I'll walk Alex home," Kit said over her shoulder. "To the pound, that is."

"Now, where's this library?" Alex asked, giving Kit's hand another pull. She looked up into Frederica's face. "I'm glad you invited me to tea."

"I am, too." Frederica's wrinkles and her big smile made her look just like a grandmother should look. As the three walked down a very long, very wide hallway, Alex let herself imagine how they must look together. Kind of like grandmother, mother and daughter. "Do you have any grandchildren?"

"No, my dear." The old woman's smile grew just a tiny bit smaller. "I don't have any children or grandchildren." Her smile grew bigger again. "That's a good reason to cultivate new friends."

"Dad is my best friend. And books. Travel books most of all."

"Well, then, you will love my library. Ah, here we are."

They stopped in the doorway of the most amazing room Alex had ever seen. It was two stories high and filled from floor to ceiling with books and globes and pictures and stuffed animals—not the baby kind, but once real—and spooky masks and things Alex couldn't even put a name to. Halfway up the walls and running all around the room was a balcony you could get to by a spiral lighthouse staircase in one corner. There were books up there, too. Tons of books.

And sure enough, just as Frederica had said, you could get to the shelves beneath the balcony by a ladder on wheels that ran on a shiny metal track. The ceiling was painted blue with clouds, which made you think you were lying on a rock on an island, looking up into a Maine summer sky. The floor was covered in thick red and blue rugs. Next to two huge windows that looked out over the harbor islands was the biggest desk Alex had ever seen. Even Ms. Simmons didn't have a bigger one. There was a gigantic fireplace, but no fire. Someone had put a big bouquet of flowers in the opening. Pulled up next to the fireplace were two enormous leather chairs, a whopping big sofa and a table loaded with food. Lots of food. It seemed Frederica liked everything super-sized.

"Wow!" Alex squeezed the others' hands.

"Ditto," Kit whispered, returning the squeeze.

Bitsy the dog sprinted ahead of them to settle on a cushion in the sun near the windows.

"I'm so glad you like my little hidey-hole," Frederica declared. "When I'm ensconced here, I can sometimes forget the mess we often make of the outside world." The old woman slipped her hand from Alex's, then stepped to the table of food. "Come. Sit, please. Karen's tea table has no equal."

"Who's Karen?" Alex asked, sitting in a chair so big and butter-soft she sank into it and felt swallowed alive.

"She's my housekeeper."

Housekeepers in stories like *The Secret Garden* always seemed so grumpy. "Will she mind if I look at stuff?" In particular, Alex wanted to see the giant shield and spear standing in one corner of the balcony.

"No, she won't mind." Frederica perched on the sofa, smiled and poured a cup of tea, which she placed in front of Kit. "In fact, there's nothing in this room you may not look at—or touch—as long as you're as careful as you would be with your own things."

Alex liked that this lady treated her more like an adult than a kid. Liked it that Frederica didn't talk down to her. Used big words even. Lots of adults didn't bother to find out that Alex loved big words.

Pouring a cup of tea for Alex, she motioned to a three-tiered platter. "Goodies, ladies? I guarantee there's not a fat-free item among the lot!"

Alex popped a tiny sandwich in her mouth. Lobster. Her favorite. And with the crusts cut off. Yum! Reaching for another, she wondered how much she had to eat to be polite before she could explore this way-cool room. As great as the food was, the room was even better. Just made for an adventurer.

Kit glanced around. "You said this was your hidey-hole from the outside world, but I notice you have a phone, a fax and a computer."

"And a PDA. Amazing little device." Frederica offered Alex a mini chocolate éclair. "It keeps the synapses firing to remain au courant. Or at least the attempt does."

"Have you seen Kit's—Seafaring Cecil's—Web site?" Alex asked.

"I have indeed. In fact, I was so impressed with your work, Kit, I contacted my nephew Grant— actually my husband's great-nephew—who creates computer games. He's eager to meet you and discuss franchising Seafaring Cecil."

"Really?" Kit looked surprised. "I've thought of doing just that. But I'm such a loner. I'm not sure how good I'd be at collaborating."

Frederica beamed. "Well, now you have a contact. And if Grant doesn't treat you fairly, he'll have his dragon aunt to contend with."

"Great-aunt," Alex amended, licking chocolate from the corners of her mouth. "And you are. Great, that is."

"Flattery will get you everywhere, young lady. Have another sweet."

"Don't mind if I do." This time Alex helped herself to a petit four. "Then may I be excused to look around?"

"To your heart's content. But don't forget to come back to the table now and again. Kit and I can't possibly eat all this food by ourselves."

Alex gobbled the petit four, wiped her hands on her T-shirt, thought better of it and wiped them again on her napkin. Dragging her sleeve across her mouth, she grinned, then slid off her chair.

"Thanks!" she chirped over her shoulder as she made a beeline for the spiral staircase in the corner of the room.

"Charming child," Frederica murmured. "So much joie de vivre. So much curiosity. I bet you were much the same at her age."

"No." Kit felt an uncomfortable warmth rise to her cheeks. "Alex is a happy child. I was filled with rage. Even at her age."

"And why was that, if you don't mind my asking?"

Strangely, Kit didn't mind. Perhaps, because Frederica was an outsider to Pritchard's Neck. If she'd heard the sordid details of Babe's life, she wasn't letting on.

"My mother didn't want me," she answered. "Not really. And in light of what's surfaced recently, I don't know why she kept me." The admission felt like a giant stone lifted from her chest. She didn't know why she was opening up to Frederica when she'd never opened up to anyone about her childhood. Perhaps her close-to-the-chest behavior was the reason it had taken so long for her anger to diffuse, why there was still a painful splinter of rage lodged in her heart.

"What has surfaced?" Frederica asked gently.

Digging in a pocket in her shorts, Kit withdrew the photograph she'd looked at innumerable times in the past twenty-four hours. The little girl. So happy. The birthday cake with three candles. The parents on either side, unseen except for their protective arms crisscrossed behind the child.

"I found this." She handed the photo to Frederica, then recapped the contents of Sister Angelica's Christmas cards. "I suspect this girl is my sister. Or half sister. My mother gave her away, but three years later she kept me. Not that she was ever a mother."

Frederica's eyes misted. "How could a woman abandon two children when all I ever wanted was the chance to love one?" she said, her voice cracking.

For a moment Kit forgot her own hurt in the face of the older woman's. "Why did you never adopt? With adoption, I suspect my sister got the better life."

"I would have loved adopting a child, but, if my dear husband had one fault, it was that he would only allow for a child of his own bloodline."

Kit felt a catch in her throat. "Sometimes blood ties are the biggest disappoint—"

"Hey! Why are you two so gloomy?" Alex had come back, holding a small leather box bound in brass.

"Oh, my! A friend sent me that," Frederica replied, quickly dabbing at her eyes. "It's the material to create *mehndi*. But I don't know how to apply it."

"I do!" Kit exclaimed, brightening. "It's so beautiful."

"What's *mehndi?*" Alex asked.

"It's a form of body decoration used in many parts of the world. Mostly by women." Kit opened the box Alex offered. "Made with henna, it's temporary. Used for special occasions."

"Tea is a special occasion," Alex declared. "Can we use it now?"

"Why not?" Frederica smiled broadly, all trace of sadness gone. "Kit, you shall be our teacher."

"I'd love to, but perhaps we should ask Alex's father first."

"You said it's not permanent," Alex replied, already laying out the materials on the tea table. "It's not like we're gonna pierce anything. Dad'll be okay with it."

"I think it will be fun," Frederica insisted, helping Alex create more space at the table. "You know how girls prick their fingers to become blood sisters? Well, we'll become *mehndi* sisters. Much prettier. Much less painful."

"Yeah," Alex agreed. "So what part of us do we decorate?"

"Hands are the most traditional. Palms of the

hands." Kit hated to admit it, but the corny concept of becoming *mehndi* sisters with Alex and Frederica appealed to her. Surely Sean wouldn't disapprove of a little temporary, all-natural henna. "But I can only do one person at a time."

"Then the other person will entertain us by reading," Frederica suggested.

"Got any good books?" Alex stared at the two women stone-faced. "Hey, guys, that was a joke!" she declared, gesturing in circles to indicate the hundreds of volumes surrounding them.

The three laughed in spontaneous appreciation.

"In fact," Frederica said, rising, "I have just the book for three adventurous women. Alex, have you read *A Wrinkle in Time* by Madeline L'Engle?"

"Nope."

Kit grinned. "Then you are in for a treat."

"Absolutely!" Frederica exclaimed, pulling a much-worn book from a shelf.

Suddenly, Kit realized that she could get used to this girl-bonding

TWO AND A HALF HOURS after leaving Alex, Sean stood once again on Frederica Harpswell's veranda. Kit had promised to bring Alex to the pound, but he'd seen neither hide nor hair of them. Exactly how long did tea take?

Alex and he needed to stop at Brad's to welcome Emily and Eric home from the hospital. Then he had to feed Alex before heading over to Kit's to fix that railing.

"Hello." A woman in an apron answered his ring at the front door. "What can I do for you?"

"I'm here to pick up Alex McCabe. I'm her father."

"Come on in." She opened the door, then motioned for him to follow.

He inhaled sharply. Was that incense?

The woman eyed him sideways in that inscrutable New England manner that could be taken for wry humor or displeasure. "Oh, Lordy, what those women have been up to."

His heart sank. Letting Alex loose with Kit might not have been a good idea.

The woman led him down a long hallway, then stopped before a set of open double doors. "In here," she murmured, then left.

Sean took in the sight before him.

Neither Alex, nor Kit, nor Frederica noticed his arrival. So engrossed were they in what they were doing that they appeared to be captured in a painting.

On one end of a huge leather sofa, Kit sprawled, with what looked like a beekeeper's hat plopped crookedly on her head. The netting that swirled from its crown covered her face and shoulders, but Sean could see that her body was utterly relaxed, her fingers languidly playing with the netting, her shapely tanned legs stretched out before her, with those crazy red high-top sneakers on her feet. She was listening to Frederica, who sat in the center of the sofa, reading a book aloud. Gone was the big flowered hat. Instead, the regal woman's silver hair was inexpertly braided and interspersed with flowers and what looked like chopsticks. Cuddled up next to her was Alex, her face nearly hidden by a large pair of aviator goggles. She clutched a taxidermied bufflehead duck with one arm, and Frederica's little lap dog with the other.

Enthralled. There was no other word for it. His daughter was enthralled in a way only he ever got to see. Alex's teachers never saw it. Certainly the town gossips never saw it. Neither did his family much of the time. And, now, Kit and Frederica had somehow caught the magic of Alex's undivided attention.

The air was thick with the sound of Frederica's voice and the smell of incense. Sean cleared his throat.

"Dad!" Alex held up her left hand. "Look! We're *mehndi* sisters!"

Grinning, Kit and Frederica held up their left hands, too. It looked as if all three of them had dipped their palms in wharf tar.

"What the—"

"Don't worry," Kit said quickly, pushing the netting up and over her hat so that she looked like a wild outdoorsy bride. "The henna will flake off as it dries, and we'll all have beautiful red designs on our hands."

He felt a rush of protective anger. "You tattooed my daughter?"

"It's not permanent. It's painted on." Kit rose with a fire in her eyes to match his outrage. "It's all natural. It will wash off and fade—"

"You bet it will wash off, as soon as we get home." He glared at Kit. "Alex, we're leaving."

"Dad, stop!" Alex stood, but stayed near the sofa and the two women. "You need to hear what I learned today," she said in a firm, clear voice. "'Cause I learned a lot."

"Your daughter is a wonderful student, Sean," Frederica declared. Now, there was a sentence Sean had never heard at parent-teacher conferences. "Gifted, I might hazard." She paused. "And Kit is a wonderful teacher. She has a thirst for knowledge and a joyful way of imparting it to others. I, too, learned a lot today." She cast him a meaningful look.

Taking advantage of his momentary loss of words, his daughter rushed him. "We learned all about *mehndi* and how it's for special occasions and I learned about taxidermy and about African tribal masks and Frederica has the biggest vocabulary of anybody I know and we're reading *A Wrinkle in Time,* which is a way-cool book that you would love, and Frederica says I can come back any time and she'll help me put together a scrapbook journal about all the things I learn just from her library and I'm gonna pass it in to my teacher for extra credit and—"

Sean couldn't believe his ears. Maybe, just maybe, he needed to divert all that energy he'd been using to push Kit away into convincing her to stay. In Pritchard's Neck. Near his daughter. Near him.

Sean glanced across the top of Alex's head as she rolled on in her jubilant litany, and caught Kit's wary gaze. For the first time in six years, he allowed himself to want a woman. The woman, if truth be told, he'd never stopped wanting.

CHAPTER NINE

SOMETHING HAD CHANGED.

In the rosy glow of the setting sun, Kit sat on the top step of Babe's porch and watched Sean stride across the front yard, carrying his toolbox. She was expecting him—he'd promised to fix the porch railing this evening. No surprises there. But something in his posture, something in his facial expression was different. He didn't seem reluctant or closed. On the contrary, he seemed almost cheerful.

"Had a good day, McCabe?"

"Can't say as I have." He plunked his toolbox on the ground, placed his boot on the step between her feet, then crossed his arms over his raised knee so that his face was inches from her own. His hair was still damp. He'd obviously just showered and shaved, and Kit caught a whiff of scent. Faint, but unmistakable. Fresh. Masculine. Appealing.

"My boat needs a new winch," he said. "Expensive sucker. Jonas cut himself while working on the pound, and Pop had to take him to the emergency room for stitches. They lost a half day's work. Then Emily just now chewed me out for letting Alex near the baby with that God-awful looking junk you tattooed her with—although most of the stuff flaked off all over the inside of my truck." He grinned as if he were talking about someone else's troubles.

"And you're smiling because?"

"Let's say—" he looked at her as if he might devour her whole "—I think I can fix a railing without screwing up. And I guess I'm looking forward to doing something right."

"Oh. Okay. I...took apart the broken section." Flustered, she tried to stick to the official reason for his visit. "I saved some of the parts." She cleared her throat. "The original isn't fancy, as you can see. But I'm afraid some of the pieces were beyond saving."

She felt warm under his unflinching gaze, and prayed she wouldn't blush like a schoolgirl.

One corner of his mouth rose in that sexy, crooked smile. "Let me take a look." Leaning, he gazed over her shoulder at the pieces she'd stacked on the porch. "Hmm."

Hmm, indeed. His proximity, his sheer maleness made her run hot and cold. And, worse, she suspected he knew it did.

Finally, after what seemed like ages to Kit, he

backed away, then climbed the steps to examine the pathetic pile that had once been the railing.

"I brought some standard-size lumber. From the pound." He still wore that smile. Still seemed at ease. As if right here, with her, was where he wanted to be. Fixing a dumb old broken-down house. Go figure. "It's in the truck," he added.

"Do you want me to get it?" she asked, trying to focus on the project, and not the way Sean moved around her personal space. As if he had a right. What he had was a rugged grace—unpretentious, all male—that made her pulse skip.

"I don't know yet." He moved the railing parts to one side, then laid the salvageable pieces of wood like a puzzle on the rough flooring. His hands—big, long fingers, with a dusting of dark hair on the back—were work-roughened but agile. As he worked with his head lowered, a lock of hair fell over his forehead. His thick hair was dark, but days out in the sun on the open water had bleached the tips, giving him a sexy, punk look.

"I'll get the lumber." Sean's voice snapped her out of her fog. He reached in his pocket, then withdrew a twenty-dollar bill, which he thrust in her hand. "You can pay the pizza guy."

"Pizza?"

"Yeah. I ordered it before I came." Sean nodded

at a teenager getting out of a car on the road. "Carpenters have to eat. There's beer in the cooler in the bed of my truck."

Kit didn't move. Couldn't speak.

"What?" Sean grinned. "Frederica's tea fill you up? I don't know about you, but I can eat pizza as a between-meal snack."

His new casual manner nearly undid her. She hadn't anticipated this easy, companionable McCabe.

"It's just…" It's just that she wasn't used to being taken care of in any way, shape or manner.

"It's just that I'm starving," she finally said. "Great minds must think alike."

She paid for the pizza, then, avoiding Sean's gaze, unloaded the small cooler of beer.

"They were all out of snails, fried ants and blowfish, so I ordered pepperoni," he said, meeting her back at the porch.

Kit slid the pizza box onto the top step, trying to appear nonchalant about this man's simple generosity. "Alex would be disappointed to see me eating such an ordinary pizza."

"Nothing you do disappoints Alex. She's declared you her friend, and that's that."

"She's one amazing kid. Think she could take time off from school to run for president? Head up the UN? Accept a Nobel Peace Prize?" It was easy to talk to Sean about Alex. "You've done a great job raising her."

"Thanks," he said, lowering himself to the step. "That's the best thing anyone could say to me."

"Even someone who knows zip about child rearing?"

"You know more than you give yourself credit for." He scooped up a slice of pizza and handed it to her. "You raised yourself, didn't you?"

"Why don't I get all bent out of shape when you say it?"

"I'm not judging you. Just stating a fact." Not taking his gaze from hers, he lifted his slice of pizza in salute. "You've done a great job raising yourself, Ms. Darling."

"Thanks." She bit into her pizza, hoping he didn't notice her discomfort. What was with him tonight?

"Can I ask a personal question?" Sean was watching her, his eyes dark, his gaze intense.

"I prefer questions to assumptions."

"Why do you go by Seafaring Cecil? Why take a pseudonym?"

"Why not? Many writers do."

"I don't know. I'd want everyone to know it was me behind all the accomplishments."

"Perhaps it's less about the accomplishments and more about the lifestyle. I get to live exactly the way I want. Anonymously. No one knows me. No one bugs me."

He didn't say anything.

"What? You don't believe me?"

"It sounds a little like running away. Or an insurance policy against failure."

Okay. That observation sliced too close to the truth.

He frowned as if he didn't like the way his words had come out. "Don't get me wrong. The pseudonym doesn't take anything away from your accomplishments. I just wish all these years Alex and I had been following Kit Darling instead of Seafaring Cecil."

"Would it have mattered?"

"What do you think?" He reached out as if to touch her face.

"I think we need to fix the railing before the light's gone." Her pizza slice half-finished, she rose and brushed off her shorts.

Sean watched Kit try to distance herself. That wasn't the reaction he'd hoped for. He'd thought, if they could be honest, they might have a chance of a fresh start.

Don't spook her.

Pushing the pizza box aside, he picked up a saw and rose. "So now you get to ask me a personal question," he offered casually.

She handed him an old square spindle to use for measurement. "Why didn't you ever move away?"

"You sound as if you think I'm sentenced to life in Pritchard's Neck."

"You thought so in high school."

"Life's funny how it lobs you the unexpected." He measured and cut, measured and cut, setting up a rhythm, accruing a pile of simple yet sturdy new spindles. "I found I liked lobstering. Working outdoors. The independence. Then when Jillian died…" A shadow passed over his heart. "Afterward, family became more important. For Alex's sake. I saw how moving around, climbing the career ladder has put a strain on my brother Nick and his family—especially his relationship with his wife."

She didn't reply. Instead, leaning against the front doorjamb, she seemed to be a million miles away.

Of course, she would be. Here he ran on about family and roots, and she'd spent her life deliberately distancing herself from both. He hadn't meant to make her feel uncomfortable. So much for honesty and opening up.

Toenailing the new section of railing together, he searched for a new—safer—topic of conversation. "The junk man didn't come?" He nodded at Babe's stuff still stacked on the porch.

Huffing loudly, she seemed to return to prickly

Kit mode. "He wanted me to pay him to haul the stuff away."

"So it's worthless."

"Pretty much." She crossed her arms and hugged herself against the cool evening breeze. The gesture reminded him of Alex at her most stubborn. "I'll figure some way to cart it to the dump. I didn't want Stu Hardy to think he can hold the rental deposit against the mess."

"No problem. We'll use my truck. After we come ashore tomorrow."

"I couldn't ask—"

"Hey, you're helping me out tomorrow."

"But that's different."

"Not really."

Kit remained silent, frowning. And very much apart.

He put down his hammer. "We are friends, aren't we?"

She didn't answer, and he didn't like not being able to read her. Maybe he was pushing too fast.

"Here." Trying a different tack, he hefted a new piece of railing. "Help me set this section in place."

She helped, but still said nothing.

"Much as she'd want to come," he continued, determined to break through that protective outer layer of Kit's silence, "we can't take Alex. To the dump. She's a pack rat." He motioned to the pile at the end of the porch. "She wouldn't let you throw away half this stuff. Would have most of it in her tree house before you could blink."

"I actually have something for her. From this stuff," Kit replied finally. "The Seafaring Cecil scrapbook she found."

"The one your mother kept? Don't you want to keep it?"

"No." When she saw the railing was securely in place, she backed toward the door. "Plus, I found your cell phone. I'll get them both." Abruptly, she disappeared into the house.

Unsettled, he finished up the repair, then collected his tools. The whole job had taken less than an hour. The pizza and beer were virtually untouched. And now it looked as if Kit was handing him his hat, his coat and a firm good-night. So much for fresh starts.

He walked with his tools to the truck. Was he wrong to think that Kit might be the woman Alex needed in her life? The woman for him? Was he wrong to think he could convince her to stay when a whole town had pressured her to leave?

Turning, he saw her on the porch, standing in the lowering dusk. Her arms wrapped around the old scrapbook, one hand clutching his phone, she watched him with a look that verged on trust, that teetered on want.

"Here they are." She came forward to where he stood next to the truck.

She had on less makeup than that first day he'd seen her. Her skin had a healthy, natural look in the soft light, but her generous mouth seemed unnaturally tense. He wished he could put a big easy smile on her face.

"Thank you." She handed him the scrapbook and the phone. "For your help with the railing."

He caught her hands. "I'm not going away, Kit."

She stepped back, pulled her hands behind her back. "But I am."

"I'm going to try my damnedest to convince you otherwise."

"Why?" She looked stricken.

"Because I've never met anyone like you. Because I couldn't forget you."

Her eyes widened. "We want entirely different things in life."

"I don't think so." Slipping the scrapbook and the phone through the open truck window, he turned back to her.

Panic shot through Kit as Sean touched her cheek. But he felt so good—so warm, so strong—that she didn't move away. In the instant she let down her guard, he pulled her close, lowered his mouth to hers and kissed her with an intensity that shook her. She couldn't have moved if she'd wanted to.

Kissing him was heaven. Unambiguous heaven. There was no friendship in this kiss. Only want. And need.

And belonging.

She felt the hard planes and surfaces of him. His heart thundering in his broad chest. The heat of his skin through his shirt.

When she opened her mouth to him, curling her arms around his neck, he groaned softly and cupped her bottom, pulling her so close her toes merely grazed the ground. Pulling her into his passion, and, for once in her life, she didn't hit the brakes.

He dragged his mouth from hers, then breathed huskily in her ear, "We have unfinished business, you and I. Alex wants us to be friends. I want us to be more. Much more."

That's when she pulled away. "I can't stay here."

"Won't."

"Same thing." She crossed her arms and tried not to be seduced by the warmth and the strength of him. The passion of his kiss.

"You think we're different, Kit. That's it. But a part of me is just like you. Envies you," he said softly, drawing her back to him. She let him embrace her and felt like a thief stealing a little time in his arms.

"Why?" She rested her head on his shoulder and

marveled that he felt so solid. So rooted. "Why would you envy me?"

"I envy your ability to walk away whenever you want."

She tensed in his arms.

"I'm not criticizing you," he said, stroking her hair. "Far from it. Just look at you now, trying to make your mother's mess right. But, Babe aside, you've created a world where you're responsible for yourself and nobody else. It's just you and the open road. You're free. That's hard for me to compete with."

She pulled away enough to look him in the eyes. "Remember what Janis Joplin said about freedom."

With the pad of his thumb, Sean stroked her cheek. "Then what are you afraid of?"

"What am I afraid of?" She backed out of his arms. "I'm afraid of turning out like my mother. A fickle lover and an irresponsible parent."

There, she'd said it. Gulping air, she tried to quiet her racing heart.

"Ah, Kit. You are not and never will be your mother."

"How do you know?"

"Trust me." Trust. What a loaded word.

"We'll see," she replied warily.

"We'll start tomorrow. On the water." He grinned. "A sternman has to trust the captain."

Tomorrow. She'd almost forgotten her promise to sub in.

Tomorrow.

What a wonderful, scary word.

"You still want me to work for you?" she asked.

"Oh, yeah." He leaned down and captured her mouth in a long, slow, sensuous kiss. "That and about a dozen other things," he murmured against her lips.

Drawing back, he winked, then got in his truck, leaving her standing in the yard, grinning like a fool at the myriad possibilities.

WATCHING THE FIREFLIES in her backyard, Emily sat in a big white wicker rocking chair—a welcome-home present from Brad—and counted her blessings. Tried to be happy. Eric was asleep, for the time being, in his cradle upstairs. Brad was supervising the other kids' bath and bedtime routine. Her family was healthy. She was healthy. And she was loved. Even respected in the community.

Community respect. Although not a "native" of Pritchard's Neck, she came from a wealthy Maine family with plenty of statewide connections. So why had Kit Darling and Alex been invited to tea with Frederica Harpswell and not her and her girls? The question rankled.

She wasn't upset so much for herself as for her

girls. Nina and Olivia were well mannered beyond their years. She'd seen to that. They could sit still in church. They were cute and utterly feminine, a fact that more than one adult had noted…. It wasn't logical. It wasn't fair.

Who had the connection to Mrs. Harpswell? Sean? He'd never mentioned it. Alexandra herself? Hardly. Kit? Unthinkable.

"Mommy, look!" Six-year-old Olivia's piping voice interrupted Emily's brooding. "Bear is all dressed up. To say, 'Welcome home!'"

Emily turned to see her younger daughter all scrubbed and fresh in a clean nightgown, holding aloft her favorite teddy bear dressed to the nines in frilly doll clothes and what looked like real jewelry. From Emily's own collection. Despite herself, Emily smiled. Her child had good taste.

"Thank you, Olivia." She reached for the toy. "Dressing Bear up for me was very thoughtful. But before you borrow something that belongs to someone else—" she removed the opal-and-pearl ring that acted as Bear's bracelet "—you must ask permission. Do you understand?"

"Yes, Mommy." Olivia looked down.

"I'm not angry with you, honey." Emily pulled her daughter onto her lap, then gently caught her chin, turning it so that they were face-to-face. "But Mommy's jewelry is special. Your grandmother gave me this ring. It was hers. And her mother's. I'll give it to you one day."

She removed the diamond posts Olivia had pierced through Bear's ears. "And these my father gave me when I graduated from high school. I'll give them to Nina on her graduation day."

She unwound the string of pearls that Olivia had made into a crown atop Bear's head. "Maybe I'll give these to Noah's bride."

Olivia giggled. "But he's not even married!"

"Oh, I bet he will be. One day." The thought filled Emily's heart with pride and trepidation.

"And what about this, Mommy?" Olivia pointed to the gold locket she'd wrapped around Bear's neck. "Where did you get this?"

Emily felt tears rise as she fingered the delicately scrolled *E* on the locket. "This was given to me by my great-aunt Elizabeth," she said. "It was hers when she was a girl. She gave it to me when I was little because we both had names that started with the letter *E*."

But the gesture went much deeper than that. Emily only appreciated it later in life. When she was older. When she could understand that, in bestowing a family heirloom, great-aunt Elizabeth, the matriarch of the Chesterton family, had bestowed a mantle of legitimacy and belonging on Emily. Adopted, Emily would never, ever forget that family was the most important thing in the world.

Emily slipped the locket off Bear and clasped it around her own neck. She would wear aunt Elizabeth's gift to Sunday's party to remind herself.

CHAPTER TEN

WHY, EXACTLY, DID SHE HATE this place?

For a moment Kit couldn't remember as she stood on the wharf behind Sean's pound and breathed in the pale beauty of the predawn harbor. A fine mist rose from the surface of the opalescent water. Lobster boats tugged at their moorings, and at Kit's sense of adventure.

Was Sean the adventure?

She'd barely slept last night and welcomed this chance alone to compose herself.

In only a few days this man had gotten under her skin and had her reevaluating what exactly made her hate her hometown. She was reluctant to admit the edges of that hatred had begun to fray.

For a taciturn man, he'd said so many things to her last night. He'd reached out with honesty and had caught her off guard.

She'd never let anyone get close enough to say things Sean had. Sometimes, when she felt most vulnerable, she wondered if Babe hadn't ruined her for men.

"You're ahead of schedule." Sean's voice rumbled softly behind her.

A newly familiar jolt of excitement rippled through her as she turned to face him. "Hey," she said, suddenly shy. "So what do we do now?"

He smiled as if reading a double meaning into her question. "We could—"

"First we gotta put on life jackets," Alex declared emerging from the pound, dragging two vests.

"Hey, Alex!" Kit replied with a tremendous sense of relief. "I didn't know you were coming with us."

"Just try and stop me!" Alex thrust a vest in Kit's hands. "I'm not going to miss a day of lobstering with Seafaring Cecil."

"What about the suspension?" Kit turned to Sean. "I don't want to cause any trouble."

"Believe me, Alex learns as much on the water as she does in the classroom. But as a precaution, I called her principal last night and got clearance."

"Hey, I gotta come," Alex piped up. "With you working the stern, someone has to take pictures for Seafaring Cecil." Rummaging in her overalls, she produced a disposable camera. "Starting now." She aimed. "Say, cheese!" She clicked before either Kit or Sean had time to respond.

"Seafaring Cecil, meet Candid Camera." Sean winked at Alex, then nodded at the vest in Kit's hands. "Suit up."

Kit noticed his lack of safety device. "You don't wear one?" She slipped her arms in hers.

"Most lobstermen and their sternmen don't. The law states life preservers have to be on board. Wearing one is going to make your job today harder, no doubt." He hefted a cooler into a dinghy tied up at the wharf. "But I'm not risking losing my two favorite girls."

Now, why did that faintly patronizing remark make her grin?

"You're going to have to wear a pair of Jonas's old boots," he continued, pointing to a pair of boots sitting on the wharf like a pair of big, black Maine dogs. "Jonas has the smallest foot size in the family, besides Alex. We stuffed the toes with newspaper."

"Put Kit in the way you put me in, Dad!" Alex squealed.

"Shall we?" The mischief in Sean's eyes made Kit back away.

But not fast enough.

With a broad swooping motion, he wrapped his strong arms around her, pinning her arms to her side. Effortlessly, he lifted her off her feet, swung her around once, then settled her down into the rubber boots. She barely had time to inhale and exhale once before he released her and stood back, looking immensely pleased with himself.

Alex giggled. "Cool, huh?"

Cool. And hot. All at once.

"Okay, crew, we have traps to haul. Into the punt." Sean untied the small rowboat and held it steady as Alex, then Kit boarded and sat on the wooden slats that served as seats—Alex in the bow, Kit in the stern. Barely causing the boat to rock, Sean lowered himself onto the middle seat while pushing the boat away from the wharf in one fluid motion.

Without speaking, he set the oarlocks in place, pulled a worn pair of oars from under the seats and began to row out into the middle of the harbor where the *Alexandra* was moored.

Neither he nor Alex seemed to feel the need to speak, and the silence calmed Kit. She watched the mist rise and the sky turn rosy as the sun edged over the horizon. Watched the gulls wheeling above the boats, some of which were already heading down the harbor and out to sea. Watched the little eddies of current the oars made in the water's surface with every dip and stroke. Watched Sean's muscles, covered only by a worn T-shirt, ripple with the effort of rowing. Glanced at his face to find him watching her. She blushed. He smiled. And suddenly hometown didn't seem like a dirty word.

Within minutes they were alongside the *Alexandra,* a gleaming white lobster boat, about thirty-five feet long, bristling with antennae and sharp with electric-blue trim. Kit had enough experience with boats to guess her draft at three feet.

Sean slipped the oars beneath the seats while Alex used a stubby hook to snag the line that anchored the bigger boat. Expertly, she clipped the punt's line to the floating buoy, Sean's anchorage marker.

"All aboard." Grasping the gunwale, Sean held the punt steady. He looked pointedly at Kit. "Need help?"

"I'm good." Placing both hands on the gunwale, Kit raised herself as if from a swimming pool, then pivoted over the side, trying not to land on the deck like a flopping mackerel, or worse, a landlubber. As Sean's sternman today, she needed to prove herself as someone who could hold her own, take care of herself. She knew enough about the water to put on a credible show.

Alex quickly followed. "I get to start 'er up," she exclaimed. "Come watch!"

"Don't be nervous." Sean's voice sounded close behind Kit. Too close. "She's a natural with machines."

"Doesn't she need a license or something?" Kit was less concerned about an eight-year-old piloting the boat than about standing so close to her father.

Lowering the cooler onto the deck, he chuckled. "She only gets to start her. I take over from there." He moved into the wheelhouse where his daughter stood on a wooden crate, flipping toggle switches like a pro. The boat's engine roared to life in all its diesel glory.

The primitive thrumming beneath Kit's feet reminded her of watery jungle drums. Neptune blessing this venture, perhaps. It felt good to stand on the deck with a powerful rhythm massaging the soles of her feet, with the rising sun on her face and seagulls freewheeling overhead. It felt adventurous and liberating. Kit smiled. Sean had a satisfying open-air career not that different from her own. Plus, he had the bonus of home and hearth. A sweet deal if you could get it.

"Kit!" Alex's voice broke her reverie. "Come watch Dad and me navigate the harbor!"

Kit cautiously made her way around barrels and boxes and empty net bags into the wheelhouse. The interior of the boat was scuffed, but remarkably clean and shipshape. Alex stood on her crate, her hands on the wheel, while Sean stood behind her with his big hands right next to his daughter's small ones. Kit braced herself in the opposite corner.

"Watch!" Alex exclaimed. With confidence, she put the big boat in gear and gently opened up the throttle. They began to move.

"Don't you need to weigh anchor?" Kit asked, suddenly not sure she was comfortable with a child at the helm.

"Silly!" Alex beamed. "Dad already did that while you were daydreaming back there."

Sean grinned, too, but didn't take his eyes off the tricky course he took maneuvering around the boats and buoys in the harbor.

"That's the last of the daydreaming you're allowed, Kit," he warned. "As of now, your thoughts belong to me, my boat and my lobsters. As my sternman, of course."

Kit felt a blush creep into her cheeks. "If I recall, captain, twenty percent of those lobsters belong to me today. As your sternman, of course."

"She's smart, Alex." With a satisfied look, Sean rubbed his chin against his daughter's head. "There'll be no cheating her."

Alex peered out from under her father's arm. "He's just kidding, you know. We'd never cheat you."

Kit smiled, but didn't answer.

"I know the names of all these instruments," Alex declared, pride in her voice. "Here's the oil, the temp, the alternator, the depth sounder—hey, Kit, you can't see from over there. Come closer. We won't bite."

Sliding Kit a sideways glance, Sean made an imaginary chomp with those impossibly white teeth and her pulse raced. "Let Kit get her sea legs, Alex."

"Heck, we're only going five knots, Dad." Alex ducked under Sean's arm again to catch Kit's eye. "The *Alexandra* can do twenty-three knots. Not in the harbor, of course. She's not the fastest boat, but she's pretty near the most reliable. That's what Dad always says…."

Alex's enthusiastic monologue made conversation unnecessary. It felt so good to be even a silent part of this threesome.

Again, why, exactly, did she hate this place?

Although Sean kept his hands on the wheel and his eye on the channel ahead of the *Alexandra,* his thoughts were on the woman back in the corner of the wheelhouse. Kit was resisting this day on the water with him. Deep down, he knew she felt, despite the job she'd hired on to do, that the day smacked of togetherness. But deeper down, he sensed her resistance faltering, and he hoped that, by the end of today, she'd give him a chance.

It was strange that in the few times he'd dated since Jilian's death, Alex had been the drawback. Most of the women had been looking for the white wedding and the brand-new nursery. A stepdaughter had not been an attractive add-on. But with

Kit, Alex was the draw. Now Sean needed Kit to want him.

"There's the lighthouse keeper!" Alex waved frantically. "Hi, Otis!"

Sean waved, too, as he navigated past the tall, white column that signaled a fisherman's safe return, then headed out the harbor's mouth into open water. The change brought a stiffer breeze and a clearer head. "Show Kit where to stand, squirt," he told Alex, "then start filling those bait bags."

"Okeydoke, artichoke!" Alex hopped down from her crate, grabbed Kit's hand and led her starboard-side. His daughter was never happier than when she could go lobstering with him. Add Kit to the mix, and she was in paradise.

He wasn't far from it himself.

"Put these gloves on," Alex instructed. "You're gonna stand right here. Dad's gonna haul the traps. You're gonna handle the main trap—the first one—while Dad handles the trailer. You're gonna empty the bait bag, and I'll give you a fresh one. Usually, the sternman keeps the bait bags full, but you're lucky I'm here today. Then you're gonna measure the lobsters…."

As he headed for his first buoy, Sean listened with pride to his daughter's instructional patter. She had a prodigious memory that encompassed the entire lobstering routine…and she was a problem student at school. Go figure. Maybe, he should bring Candace and Alex's teachers out on the water to show his daughter's alternative education.

Reaching over the starboard side with a gaff and hook, he hooked the buoy, then lay the gaff along the gunwale. He pulled the line from the water by hand to get enough slack to run it through the hauling block mounted forward on the bulk-head. With his left hand he operated the handle for the hauler as the line emerging from the water coiled on the deck. He tossed the buoy onto the gunwale next to the wheelhouse. When the knot joining the line to the float rope went over the block, he slowed the hauler and watched for the first familiar wire mesh trap. As it cleared the gun-wale, he shoved it toward the stern and found himself staring into beautiful fog-gray eyes. Kit's. Lost in routine, he'd almost forgotten her. How could he? She was unforgettable.

Kit made lobstering one-hundred percent more enjoyable.

"The trailer, Dad!" Alex shouted as the second trap cleared the gunwale, returning him to the business at hand.

"I'll show Kit what to do," his daughter added with a wise little smirk. "Looks like she's not the only one daydreaming."

Grinning like a schoolboy, Sean opened the

door of the trailer trap, unwound the bait bag's drawstring from the cleat and dumped the half-eaten remains overboard for the gulls. Alex took the empty bag and handed him and Kit full ones.

With a brass measure he pulled from his jeans, he measured the two lobsters in the trap. Only one was a keeper. The other was two-and-three-quarters inches from its eyes to the end of its carapace. He threw the short overboard. Banding the keeper's claws, he tossed it into a barrel of salt water. Kit and Alex had come up empty. He hoped the catch would pick up as the day went on.

"Okay, punkin—" he signaled Alex "—show Kit how to push them overboard."

He jogged the boat to starboard, watching to keep buoys out of the wheel and avoiding setting the traps over someone else's. Satisfied they were clear, he waited for Kit and Alex to push the two traps back into the water, then headed for his next buoy.

Although he could do this work in his sleep, he found lobstering brought him, not boredom, but a sense of contentment. For the next several hours, they hauled, picked, baited and set in a rhythm that felt like second nature. The day was clear, the sea relatively calm, the catch increasing. He left Kit's tutorial to Alex and hoped the woman was growing easy in his presence. It was enough for him—for now—that she was on his boat.

At eleven, he put the *Alexandra's* gearshift in Neutral. "Break out the cooler, me hearties!" he cried. "You've earned yourselves lunch!"

"You mean it's not dinnertime?" They were the first words Kit had spoken directly to him since they'd begun.

He eyed her for signs of fatigue—she'd put in a full morning's work without a word of protest—but she looked fine. More than fine, she looked happy as she leaned against the gunwale with a grin from ear to ear. But her pink nose was badly in need of sunscreen. He'd made Alex lather up before they'd left the house.

"Hold on a second." He rinsed his hands with the hose from the freshwater barrel, then pulled out a tube of zinc oxide. Before Kit could protest, he daubed a thick smear of white down the bridge of her nose. "War paint. Scares the lobsters right into the trap."

Click. Alex caught the moment on film before his finger left the tip of Kit's nose. That was a memory for the scrapbook. Especially since Kit hadn't flinched or retreated. In fact, she stood before him, her ample mouth turned up at the corners in a bemused smile, her compact body at ease, her clear gaze resting on him as if she had no intention of resisting his touch. Ah, the magic of life on the water.

"Let's eat!" Alex headed for the cooler.

"Wash those hands, kiddo." Sean reached for Kit's hands, then slowly removed her gloves.

"What—" She tried to pull away, but he hung on.

"Just checking for blisters." He turned her hands palms up. "None. Good. I don't want to drive the help off by working them to the bone."

"I'm used to hard work." Kit's eyes issued a challenge. Not a belligerent one, more teasing. "Surprised?"

"Nothing about you surprises me." That wasn't exactly true. The power she still exerted over him had come as a real surprise.

"Save it for the date, Dad," Alex suggested. "I'm hungry."

"Date?" Kit cocked one eyebrow.

"She wants us to date. What do you think?"

The *Alexandra* drifted. The radio crackled softly in the background. And time seemed to stand still as Kit held his gaze.

"Date. Hmm. That's a good one." She slipped her hands from his. "So, Alex, should we date like the Wodabe of Africa?"

Alex giggled. "How's that?"

"Along with all his buddies, a Wodabe man slathers his face, first with the milk of a white cow, then with red and yellow paint made from clay." Kit smiled coyly. "He layers on the beads and the ostrich feathers, and then he dances and sings in a

long conga line, hoping to outshine his buddies.
Hoping he'll be chosen the most handsome man.
Hoping the prettiest girl will ask him to marry."

"Could you see your old dad doing that?" Sean
asked, glad Kit was keeping the mood light. He
dipped into the cooler to pass out ham-and-cheese
sandwiches.

"No way!" Alex exclaimed, laughing. She
turned to Kit. "So, did you learn all that stuff being
Seafaring Cecil?"

"Actually, I learned about the Wodabe in a public library. Armchair traveling. Just like you and
your dad."

"Cool!"

"You bet!" Kit bit into her sandwich with gusto.
"I may never have been lobstering before today,
but from books I know that before the nineteenth
century, only widows, orphans and servants ate
lobsters."

"The pilgrims thought they were only good for
fertilizer," Alex countered, warming to this game.

"Did you know lobsters are nocturnal?"

"Did you know they're related to spiders?"

Sean chuckled. "Trivia queens. I'm surrounded
by trivia queens."

"Well, what do you want to talk about, captain?" Kit cocked her head and sent him a mischievous grin.

"I want to know what you think of your first morning on a lobster boat." That was the safest of the many things he wanted to talk about.

"Fresh air. Great exercise. No bosses peering over your shoulder. I'd say you have a good life."

"So you'd say it's possible to stay in your hometown, work and not lose your freedom?"

"Ah, McCabe, you seek to trick me." Her eyes sparkled as if she didn't mind.

"I think Pritchard's Neck is a great place for someone like Seafaring Cecil," Alex added hopefully. "To come home to between adventures."

"I'm not talking about Seafaring Cecil, necessarily," Kit replied, "but I could see where some enterprising soul could set up a small coastal kayaking operation. Guided tours. Or special outings for artists. It would be ecologically sound. And a whole lot of fun."

"Yeah!" Alex agreed. "Do it, Kit! Do it!"

"I wasn't talking about me. I was just speaking hypothetically." But she had a dreamy look in her eyes that said she was thinking about it. Which meant she was taking those first baby steps toward seeing Pritchard's Neck—and perhaps Sean—in a whole new light.

He reached for a second sandwich. The possibilities stirred up this morning had given him an enormous appetite.

ALEX COULD BARELY CONTAIN her excitement. Kit and Dad were getting along. Really getting along. Smiling. Joking. Bumping into each other accidentally on purpose. Right now, Dad was sliding the *Alexandra* alongside the pier to refuel and pick up bait for tomorrow before heading back to their mooring behind the pound. Kit was standing right next to him in the wheelhouse, asking questions and taking pictures with Alex's disposable camera. Both she and Dad looked happy. Oh, yeah, they were ready for a real date.

Whistling to herself, Alex hosed down the deck. They'd had a good haul and had left the lobsters at the association's floating car, in crates with Dad's buoy tied to them. The association managers needed to weigh and record them. Dad should be pleased. Alex knew he needed the money to finish the pound. And Kit's twenty percent should make up for the crummy yard sale. The two of them sure looked pleased right now. Side by side.

Maybe after they gassed up, Alex could suggest Kit come over for supper. Or better yet—as Dad's date—for the party on Sunday. For supper tonight Alex could give the invitation, but for Sunday— for it to be a date—she had to find some way for her dad to think of asking. She would. As happy as he now looked, he was open to suggestion.

"Hey, Alex!" Kit aimed the camera her way. "Say, cheese!"

"Mozzarella!" Alex shouted with a happy heart.

"Kit Darling." From the pier a man dressed in fancy clothes peered over the side of their boat. "I'm Grant Harpswell. My aunt said you'd be coming in on the *Alexandra.* We saw you through her telescope." He held out his hand for Kit to shake or to give her a boost ashore. "Is this a bad time? I really want to talk about Seafaring Cecil, but unfortunately I'm not in town long…."

Alex clenched her teeth. Kit didn't need big money. She had twenty percent of Dad's catch today. Plus, she could go out as his sternman any time she wanted more. Alex looked to her dad for support, but he was going about business as usual. He was used to tourists watching him work, and, more often than not, he tuned them out.

But Alex knew this guy was no ordinary tourist. He was after their Kit.

"That was quick." Kit moved toward the man, actually shook his hand across the gunwale. But she didn't go ashore. Good. "Frederica told me you'd be in touch, but I never expected so soon."

"Hey, you know what they say about the early bird. My aunt has a keen eye for a good business deal. When she told me about you, I drove right up from Boston." When he smiled, Alex thought he looked like a ferret. She didn't trust him. Especially not with Kit. "Are you finished here? Can we talk? I'll buy you a cold drink."

Oh, no! If Kit left now, she wouldn't get a chance to invite her to supper or the family picnic.

"Can you come eat with us tonight?" Alex blurted even before asking Dad. "We can have lobsters 'cause you helped catch 'em."

Kit looked at Frederica's nephew, then at Dad who was changing out empty bait barrels for fresh. Dad needed to stop working for a minute and realize this new guy could mean competition.

"Mr. Harpswell—"

"Grant."

"Grant has driven all the way up from Boston. If I understand what he's offering, we have a lot to talk about. It could take a while, Alex."

"Then maybe you could come to our family picnic on Sunday." Alex moved to her dad's side and tugged his pocket. "Say something!" she hissed.

Dad looked at Mr. Harpswell and finally seemed to realize he had the power to take Kit away. "I'd like you to come to the picnic," he said to Kit. "My brother and his family are moving back to town. I have a feeling you and Chessie would hit it off. She's a potter and a free spirit."

Alex would have rather Dad talked less about Aunt Chessie and Kit hitting it off and more about how Dad and she had hit it off today. How Dad wanted to see more of her. Mushy stuff even. Anything to convince her.

"I...I don't know." Kit looked torn. "Depending on how things go this afternoon, I might be able to leave by Sunday."

Gee, this was not how things were supposed to work out. Dad needed to do or say something. Loud and fast. Instead, he said, real quiet-like, "You know how I feel about that."

It wasn't the smoothest line in Alex's opinion, but it made Kit pause. "Yeah," she said, blushing under her zinc oxide stripe. "I do."

Slick and ferrety, Mr. Harpswell cleared his throat.

"I need to consider this offer," Kit said at last.

"I know." Dad gave her a boost—actually gave her a boost as if he were giving her to this new guy—from the boat to the pier. "Let me know how it turns out."

"You bet."

She looked a little sad to go, but that didn't make Alex feel any better. She went. With a guy not Dad. To talk about Seafaring Cecil—something she could do to her heart's content with them. Over supper.

Fighting back tears, she leaned into her dad. "Why'd you let her go? Why didn't you do something to make her stay?"

"If you try to make Kit do something, sweet

pea, she's going to do the opposite." Dad stroked her hair with his big comforting hand. "If she's going to trust me, I've got to let her do what she's got to do."

"Do you like it?"

"Not a bit."

"Are you gonna figure a way to make what she's gotta do involve us?"

"Promise."

Alex felt better. Her dad didn't make promises he couldn't keep.

CHAPTER ELEVEN

SUNDAY AFTERNOON Sean sat on Emily and Brad's stoop and watched the cousins playing kick ball in the front yard while the adults mingled in the back. Nick, Chessie and the girls had arrived in town last night. They planned to stay with Pop, Jonas, Sean and Alex for a week while they closed on their new house and registered Isabel and Gabriella for school. This morning over breakfast, the brothers had had a chance to catch up. So now, Sean had escaped the grown-up party, knowing full well Emily wanted him to chat up her cousin from Portland.

He didn't mean to be rude and although Wendy Chesterton seemed nice enough his thoughts were on Kit. Kit, whom he'd seen in town in Grant Harpswell's Ferrari.

He didn't know why that should bother him, but it did.

Maybe because Harpswell had money—a powerful aphrodisiac—something Sean was short of at the moment. Frederica's nephew was also a mover and a shaker, someone who could talk Kit's out-of-the-box lingo. Sean had learned to like the box and wished Kit could, too. That damn Ferrari. A grown-up cousin to Kit's Harley, it spelled fast times and moving on.

Here it was Sunday and he'd had no word from her on any deal she and Harpswell might have struck. Not that Kit needed to keep him informed. But he sure would like to know if she'd earned herself a quick ticket out of town.

"Not so close to the road," he called to the kids.

Nick's girls had joined the cousins today. Isabel was sixteen and Gabriella thirteen, but you couldn't tell their ages now as they whooped and romped with the younger ones as if they were peers. Despite the older girls' ages, he didn't know if he could count on them to act responsibly. If they all needed supervision, so much the better. He'd volunteer. Sitting out here with the kids was better than trying to fend off Emily's matchmaking maneuvers.

"Gabriella! Aim your pitch more toward the driveway, not the road," he admonished.

"There you are!" Emily rounded the corner of the house. "We all wondered where you'd gone. Especially Wendy."

"The kids get lost in the game and don't watch for traffic."

"So I'll watch them." Emily beamed up at him, obviously enjoying being the hostess. Queen bee. "You go back to the adults. Nick and Chessie haven't seen you in ages. And Wendy wants to get to know you better."

"Sorry, Em. Wendy seems a bit Fortune 500 for me."

"But you haven't—"

"Alex! Noah! Stop!" Sean saw the ball go out in the street. Saw the two cousins lost in competition to retrieve it. Saw the big vintage Mercedes approaching. "Stop! Now!"

He sprinted across the lawn.

The squeal of tires galvanized Emily. "Oh, no!" she shrieked, racing after Sean, who had scooped up both Alex and Noah from the middle of the road. The Mercedes had skidded to a stop, angled up onto the neighbors' lawn across the street. The driver, Grant Harpswell, leaped from the car.

"I'm so sorry!" he exclaimed. "They came out of nowhere. Are they all right?"

"Are you all right, sweetie?" Emily grabbed Noah from Sean.

"They're both okay." Sean's reply was curt as he focused on the other cousins gathering round. "And a lot wiser." He leveled a grim look at the children. "Do you understand how bad a situation this could have been? How alert you have to be when you play in the front yard?"

"You warned them," six-year-old Olivia offered primly.

"I warned all of you, sweetheart."

"I'm so sorry," Grant Harpswell repeated.

"It wasn't your fault." Sean gave the man a cool once-over before turning his attention to his passengers—Kit and Frederica—now hurrying across the street.

From her perch in Sean's arms, Alex spied Kit. His daughter brightened even as Sean saw Emily's face drop. "It was our fault, mister," Alex offered. "And we're sorry. Maybe we could make it up to you. Wanna join our picnic?"

"That's very sweet of you, dear," Frederica replied, "but we were just on our way to lunch. To celebrate Grant and Kit's business agreement. I'm so sorry we've disrupted your gathering."

Sean watched conflicting emotions in Emily's face. Before her, Kit stood, with Frederica Harpswell—someone Emily would love to get to know.

"Emily," Sean said, "I don't believe you've met Frederica Harpswell, Kit Darling and Grant Harpswell. This is my sister-in-law Emily McCabe."

"It's a pleasure to meet you," Emily said, looking directly at Frederica. "Especially since no harm's been done. Are you and your car all right?"

"Yes. Yes, we're all fine. Fortunately, my nephew is an excellent driver with quick, young reflexes. We were concerned for the children."

The children, minus Alex, had begun to sneak off to begin a fresh game away from the admonishing eyes of adults.

"Alex did have a wonderful idea." Emily cast a quick sidelong glance at Kit as if she might reconsider her plan, but took a deep breath and settled into her role as hostess. "Since you were on your way to lunch, I insist you join us."

"Please, stay!" Alex wriggled from her father's arms to skip about Frederica and Kit. "Please, please, please! The food is great." Alex looked contritely up at her aunt. "I tested."

"Millicent Crenshaw catered," Emily said. Sean wasn't certain whether his sister-in-law was trying to entice Frederica or warn Kit off.

Kit stiffened. She looked at Frederica, then at Grant. "You can go—"

"It's all for one and one for all, dear heart," Frederica insisted, taking Kit's hand. "If you would prefer, we'll continue on to the White Barn Inn. All three of us."

"Please, stay." Emily looked at Sean, and something seemed to give. "All three of you."

"Stay," Sean urged. "I need a way to thank Frederica for coming up with a terrific substitute sternman." It couldn't hurt to remind Kit of the wonderful day they'd spent together on the water.

"Oh, my! It's simply delightful to be so wanted." Frederica turned to her nephew. "Well, Grant?"

Just then, Emily's cousin rounded the corner of the house. Tanned and fit and dressed to the nines in cruise wear and high-heeled sandals, Wendy oozed polished self-confidence. "So! There's an alternative party out here."

Grant's eyes brightened. "You know how I love a party, Aunt Fred." He extended a hand to Emily's cousin. "Grant Harpswell."

Wendy dimpled as she took in Grant's impeccable shoes, slacks, shirt and sweater draped elegantly around his shoulders. "Wendy Chesterton. Pleased to meet you."

As they shook hands, perfectly manicured, Sean could see the wheels in Emily's head begin to turn. Grant and Wendy would be a perfect match. In his opinion, too. With the prospect of a Harpswell-Chesterton pairing, however temporary, maybe he could convince Kit to stick around.

"Come meet the rest of the family." Emily slipped her arm through Frederica's. "I feel as if I know you already. Alex has talked nonstop about your tea party. My daughters absolutely adore tea parties…"

Alex took Kit's hand and placed it firmly in her father's. "So, Kit, I guess this is where you were s'posed to be all along." She performed an exuberant cartwheel on the lawn.

Kit looked unsure.

"She's right," Sean agreed, squeezing Kit's hand. "I told you I was going to find ways to keep you in town. Massive amounts of food seem as good a start as any."

"I am hungry." Kit took a deep breath. "It's just that big families…families in general…well, my social skills are rusty."

"You'll do fine." Sean smiled at her, fully appreciating the effort it took for her to step outside her comfort zone. "Stick with me. I've got an in."

"You won't abandon me?"

"Not a chance."

"Give me a minute to steel myself."

Alex flopped on the grass at their feet. "What's your deal with Frederica's nephew?"

"Hey, squirt—" Sean shot her a warning look "—that's none of your business."

"It's okay." Kit looked relieved. "We're going to expand Seafaring Cecil. Make it into a computer game."

"And give up the books and the Web site?" Alex said anxiously.

"No. The game will be in addition to the books and the Web site. In addition to the catalog."

"Cool!" Alex executed a series of somersaults. Then, secure in the knowledge that her hero was staying, she hopped up to chase after her cousins.

"Congratulations on the deal. Looks like all your hard work paid off." Sean felt happy for Kit. He really did. But he couldn't help wondering how fast this new enterprise would pull Kit away. "Does this mean less time on the road? More time in an office in Boston?"

"Heavens, no!" Kit looked horrified. "Grant's taking it from here with all the technical stuff. All the office and studio stuff. Although I'll have creative input. I wouldn't have signed anything that would tie me down."

That should've made him feel better but her insistent rootlessness gave Sean a knot in his stomach. "You just met Harpswell. Can you trust him?"

"Frederica assures me I can, although I do feel terribly protective of old Cecil." She shrugged. "But, in the end, I read all the fine print with the lawyer Frederica recommended, signed on the dotted line and took Grant's money."

Sean marveled that she could be so casual about what she did, where she went, how much she earned.

"Enough money, I hope," he said. His finances

were always tight. And Kit found herself in a par-
ticularly sticky situation right now with Babe's
debts. "I don't mean to pry."

"Let's just say I'll need more fingers and toes
to add it all up." She brightened, the old self-as-
sured Kit returning. "With the advance, I can take
care of Babe's mess and move on. That alone
makes it a good deal."

That didn't sound like any kind of a good deal
to Sean.

KIT WIPED HER HANDS on the elegant guest towel
and stared into the mirror of Emily and Brad's
downstairs bathroom. What was she doing here?

There was a knock on the door. "Are you all
right?" Frederica's kind voice.

Kit opened the door to face Frederica and
Alex. "I'm fine," she said although the Martha
Stewart hominess of Emily's house and the robust
camaraderie of the McCabe clan made her a little woozy.

"Perhaps we ought to leave," Frederica suggested.

"No!" The look on Alex's face showed genuine
horror.

"I just need a minute to collect my thoughts,"
Kit replied. Her thoughts, should she be so bold as
to admit to them, were less about Emily's house
and the McCabes and more about one particular

McCabe. Sean. He'd been the model of chivalry this afternoon, if a little detached.

He'd introduced her with enthusiasm to his family, staying close while steering her toward family members she might actually have something in common with—like his sister-in-law Chessie. And he'd seemed glad about her new Seafaring Cecil venture. Yet she sensed he was holding back.

"It's been a while since I've been surrounded by so many people," she said, distracted. Crowds never bothered Cecil. Intimacy, however, bothered Kit. And she could think of nothing so intimate as family. Especially when she stood on the outside looking in.

Alex took her by the hand. "Then let's go in the living room. Nobody's there right now." She led them across the hall and through an archway into a comfy room strewn with toys and books and family photographs.

"Hey!" Alex turned to Frederica. "Remember we're going to make a scrapbook of things I could learn in your library?"

"How could I forget?" Frederica smiled at Alex. "You may return any time."

"Well, I'll show you the kind of scrapbook I want to make." Alex headed for the bookshelves along one wall. "Aunt Emily makes the coolest. It's her hobby." She wrestled with a big album on one shelf.

"Are you sure your aunt would want you going through her things?" Kit asked.

"Oh, we can't touch the ones on her worktable in the laundry room. But when the albums are finished, we can look all we want. Aunt Emily says it's our heritage." Alex grinned. "Another vocabulary word."

"Let me assist you, dear," Frederica offered, helping Alex ease the big album onto the coffee table. "Oh, my. This is lovely. Look, Kit."

"Aunt Emily's a little girl in this album," Alex explained.

Kit peered over Alex's shoulder to see an album laid out with a graphic designer's eye. The pages pulled you in even if you didn't know the cast of characters. If Emily weren't so cool toward her, Kit would ask her for pointers on adding visual punch to the Seafaring Cecil Web site.

"Aunt Emily keeps everything," Alex continued. "Here's some of her hair when she was three."

Kit glanced at the page and froze. That photo.

The little blond girl stood on a chair, dressed in party finery. She blew out three candles on a cake. Her parents stood on either side, unseen except for their arms crisscrossed behind the child. She'd looked at the same image over and over in the photo Babe had kept.

Her head beginning to pound, Kit placed a trembling finger beside the photo in the album. "This is your Aunt Emily?"

"Yeah. When she was a little girl. Like I said." Alex looked up at Kit, question in her eyes. "Are you okay?"

No. She wasn't okay. Emily McCabe was her sister? Or was she crazy?

"Kit—"

She didn't stick around to hear what Frederica was about to say. She didn't care that she might appear rude, or frightened or downright nuts to Alex. She needed air. Stumbling through the house, she found the front door and pushed through. Across the yard of romping cousins. Down the sidewalk toward Babe's house. The air was sharp in her lungs. And the headache pulled at the base of her skull.

Emily McCabe was her sister.

She would never be free of Babe and her past. If she were to pursue a relationship with Sean, how could she keep such a secret from him? But if she were to tell him, what awful consequences would it have for Emily?

Emily didn't know, Kit was absolutely certain. And, as much as she didn't warm to the woman, she wouldn't wish a family intimacy with Babe on anyone.

No, Kit had to follow Babe out of Pritchard's Neck. What she needed was yet another fresh start, and her deal with Grant Harpswell would give her just that. Their contract afforded her the where-withal to straighten Babe's affairs in a few days. She could lay low long enough to do that. She didn't even have to explain herself to Sean. He couldn't possibly think a few hot kisses meant any kind of promise.

She raced across Babe's front yard and up the porch steps. A rolled up sheet of paper had been stuck between the doorjamb and the screen door. It was a fax delivered through Branson's store. She recognized Babe's loopy signature at the bottom.

Ed turned out to be a bore, the message read. *But I'm tapped. Be a love and wire me bus fare home. Send it to the following Western Union address....*

Damn it all to hell. This could not be happening.

Throwing herself against the doorjamb, Kit slid down the outside wall and collapsed on the porch. Her headache had progressed to industrial strength. Tears stung her eyes. She had worked so very hard to escape the bottomless bog her mother had dug. And now Babe wanted to use Kit, once again, to return to Pritchard's Neck and drag down a whole new set of innocents.

Not if Kit had anything to say about it. She struggled to her feet.

"Kit!" Frederica called out as she hurried after her. "Darling girl, we must talk." The octogenarian climbed the stairs to stand breathless before her. "Sean was in a lather to get to you, but I told him the matter absolutely required a woman-to-woman chat to sort it out. I'm afraid he's more determined than most. He told me he'd give me a fifteen-minute head start."

"I can't face him. Not now."

"You can't avoid him."

"You saw that picture. Do you know what it means?"

"Yes, I do."

"Once I take care of Babe's debts and figure out a way to keep her from returning, I'm out of here."

"Why do you think your mother would return?"

Kit thrust the fax at Frederica.

"Oh, my." The older woman reached out to stroke Kit's hair in a gesture so maternal Kit could no longer control the tears. "You poor thing," Frederica crooned, enveloping Kit in her arms. "You poor, beleaguered darling."

"I can't let her come back," Kit sobbed. "She has the power to unravel so many lives. I should just send her the remainder of the advance and tell her to take it and disappear."

"There, there. I'm afraid that course of action will solve nothing. Your mother will simply smell a cash cow and hang around to milk it dry." Frederica reached in a pocket to produce a clean linen handkerchief. "We'll think of something. But not here. You need a hot bath and a soft bed, neither of which you'll find in this sorry excuse for an abode. You're coming home with me. To stay. Indefinitely."

"I couldn't."

"You most certainly can. I won't take no for an answer."

Frederica placed her hands on Kit's shoulders, firmly holding her gaze. "There is nothing two intelligent women can't figure out when they put their minds together. But we need a civilized environment." Her lovely old face crinkled into a smile. "Now, collect your belongings, and Sean will drive us home. Here he comes now. I'm surprised he gave me five minutes."

"But Grant—"

"Grant and the Chesterton girl have, as they say, hooked up. I wouldn't worry about them."

Kit swallowed hard as she saw Sean get out of his truck. "I told you I can't face him."

"Of course you can. He's only a man. Even if he's head over heels in love with you."

Love? Had Kit heard correctly? Sean in love with her?

No. He couldn't possibly be in love with her. Love should mean knowing what you're getting yourself into. Sean didn't have a clue. Could he entertain the remotest possibility of Babe as Alex's step-grandmother? Or Nina's, Noah's, Olivia's and baby Eric's biological grandmother? Love meant honesty. And Kit couldn't share this secret with Sean.

If he was in love with her, he wouldn't back off. Kit would have to do that for him. For him. And for Alex. And even for Emily and her children.

As Sean climbed the steps, a worried expression on his face, Kit turned to go in. To get her backpack. To seek temporary refuge with Frederica.

She let the door slam in Sean's face.

CHAPTER TWELVE

SEAN DIDN'T GET IT.

Something had gone wrong at the party. And neither Kit nor Frederica seemed willing to fill him in.

Before starting his truck, he glanced across Frederica to where Kit sat hunched against the passenger door, shutting him out.

"Did any of my family say anything to hurt you?" he asked, too concerned to pussyfoot around. "Because if they did—"

"They didn't," Frederica assured him. Why didn't Kit answer for herself? "It's a case of too many people in too short a time." She patted his arm. "Kit just needs some space."

He didn't mind giving her space. What he minded was that she might blow town without looking back. He knew they could work out their differences, but they wouldn't have time if she gave up and left. He needed to give her a reason to stay.

But what? He only had love and a ready-made family to offer. Love. He hadn't told her how he felt. Up until now, he hadn't admitted to himself how he felt. For the past six years, love had held a narrow definition for him that included only Alex and his family. Kit had changed the definition.

And family? Well, at the moment, it looked as if family—his family—had scared the hell out of her.

In confused silence, he drove to Frederica's. The gulls wheeled above her white mansion at the water's edge in the early evening sun, and with the lighthouse in the distance, it was a postcard-perfect setting. "A safe harbor."

Until she trusted him enough to let him into her confidence, he was glad Frederica had befriended her. Kit would be safe here. And feeling safe, she might not leave Pritchard's Neck before he could convince her never to go.

Kit opened the truck door before he'd come to a full stop. She slid down from the cab and walked up the crushed-shell path as if she were carrying the weight of the world on her narrow shoulders.

"Dammit!" He slammed his fists on the steering wheel. "How can I make it right if I don't know what happened?"

"It's not a problem for you to make right," Frederica gently replied. "But I would like to talk to you. Will Alex be all right with your family if you stay a bit longer?"

"Of course." He dug his cell phone out of his pocket. "I'll call her and tell her I'll be late. But what do I tell her about Kit? She's sure to ask."

"Tell her the truth. That Kit is exhausted and needs some rest."

Sean helped Frederica from the truck. "I'll be right back," she said. "I want to see that Karen draws a hot bath for Kit. Our girl needs plenty of unconditional TLC. Wait for me on the veranda. We'll talk. And I'll try to make clear what I can."

As Frederica made her way into the house, Sean punched in Emily and Brad's number on his phone. Alex picked up on the first ring. "Dad?"

"It's me, sport. I just called to tell you Kit's going to stay at Frederica's. I drove her over, and I'm going to stay until she's settled."

"Is she okay? Aunt Emily wants to know if you think it's food poisoning."

"I don't think it was food poisoning. Otherwise, we'd all be sick," Sean replied, carefully choosing his words. "Kit's just tired. Really tired. All the work she's had to do for her mom caught up with her."

"You think we worked her too hard on the boat Friday?"

"I don't know. I hope not. But Frederica and her housekeeper are going to treat her like a princess,

I bet, so don't you worry. Kit will be back on her feet in no time."

"She'd better be 'cause Grant says he has a big surprise for her. He says it's a bonus and it's coming in a few days. He says I'm gonna love it, too."

Grant Harpswell again. And his bottomless pockets.

Sean didn't need this guy luring Kit away with big-time perks. And he sure as hell didn't need him dazzling Alex. But if this bonus would keep Kit in town a few more days, so be it.

He kept his voice even. "You sit tight, kiddo. I'll pick you up as soon as Kit's all settled in here."

"Okay, Dad. I love you."

"I love you, too."

Kit had worked her way into Alex's heart as much as she had into his. Now Kit showed every sign of moving on, leaving a big emotional gap. So what if he could convince her to stay? Would that be like caging and clipping the wings of a rare and beautiful bird? He hated to think he'd be the one to confine her.

"Sean." Frederica stood at the end of the veranda. "Don't you think we'd be more comfortable up here?"

"Sure." Shaking the tangle of what-ifs from his mind, he made his way across the lawn. "How's Kit?"

"Soaking in a hot bath." Frederica took his arm and steered him to a couple of wicker chairs with a view of the lighthouse. "She's a very strong young lady. She'll be fine."

"I know she'll be fine. She's a survivor. I'm worried she'll decide to be fine far away from Pritchard's Neck."

"I, too, have worried that very point." Frederica paused as her housekeeper arrived with a tray of tea things. "Karen, would you please bring us the cognac, instead? I believe our conversation is going to require something stiffer."

"Ayuh," Karen replied. "Two glasses or the bottle?"

"Two glasses and the bottle." Frederica's eyes twinkled as she watched her housekeeper stiffen. "Sean and I will keep our options open."

"How big a problem are we facing?" Sean asked as Karen disappeared into the house.

"I won't lie to you. Kit is very strong, but she's also very stubborn. She has it in her head that she can do more harm than good by staying in town. Our job is to convince her otherwise."

"Harm to—?"

"To Alex and you. To your family."

Guiltily, he remembered he'd thought the very same thing five days ago. "What set her off this afternoon?"

"I'm not at liberty to disclose that. In time, I hope she'll share her dilemma with you."

"How can I help if I don't know what she's facing?"

"You can let her know how you feel about her."

Easier said than done.

"Sean?"

"I'm not sure what I feel for her is enough. The reality is I'm not going anywhere. I'm rooted here with a daughter, a family, a business. What Kit needs is bigger than all that. She needs what someone like…your nephew can provide."

"Pshaw! I'm very fond of Grant, but neither he nor his considerable resources are capable of giving Kit what she needs. Or wants." Frederica leaned in with a confidential air. "Kit lacks a sense of belonging. You and Alex can provide that. But because Kit has been hurt in the past—and badly—she's created a wall of bravado around herself so that she can't be hurt again. You, sir, need to scale that wall."

"You're saying Kit needs me?"

"Yes. And she wants you. Although wanting you goes against all her instincts for self-preservation."

Kit wanted him? "So why is she shutting me out?"

"She cares for you enough that she's willing to keep the secret she's carrying and sacrifice her happiness so as not to harm yours."

"What the hell is this secret? Is it that powerful?"

"Potentially. You need to make her feel safe enough to share it even if she never does. It's a delicate issue requiring a fine touch."

"If you hadn't noticed, Mrs. Harpswell, I'm a blunt man. Finesse is not my strong suit."

"Believe me—" Frederica smiled enigmatically "—you have all the requisite skills and then some."

What had Kit gotten herself into?

At that moment, Karen returned with the cognac. Good. He needed a stiff drink.

MONDAY MORNING KIT STOOD in the middle of Babe's empty porch and watched the junk man pull away with the yard sale leftovers. She should feel relief. Relief that Grant's advance meant she could easily pay her way out of town. As soon as she ran a broom through the house and wrote a check to the consumer credit help agency, she was free to leave. Get back to Seafaring Cecil's new and improved life, as if this little detour had never happened.

But she didn't feel free to leave. Didn't she have to deal with Babe wanting to come back? Didn't she have to make a decision about her newfound sister? And could she really leave without saying goodbye to Alex? To Sean?

The thought of Sean turned her resolve to mush.

She didn't want to say goodbye to him. Her no-strings lifestyle couldn't hold the same allure it once had. What a difference a few days made.

"Need help?" Alex scampered across the front yard, her cousin Noah in tow.

"Hey, guys." Kit tried for a nonchalance she didn't feel. She pinned Alex with what she hoped was a mature adult look. "I know why you're not in school, but—" she leveled an equally serious look at Noah "—why aren't you in school?"

"I have an ear infection." Noah rubbed the side of his head. "Dad took the day off. He's gonna take me to the doctor's. In an hour."

"In an hour," Kit mused, turning again to Alex. "So, is your uncle watching you today?" She didn't want to get in trouble with the McCabes again.

"Nope. Pop Pop and Uncle Jonas are. But Pop Pop had me return a level he borrowed from Uncle Brad."

"And you're sticking around to play with Noah, why?"

Alex grinned. "You know, Kit, you could be a teacher you ask so many questions."

"Don't get smart with me, young lady." Kit grinned, too. "Now, why are you hanging with Noah?"

Alex rolled her eyes. "When I saw Noah was home, I called Pop Pop, and he said I could stay till Noah had to go to the doctor's."

"And you're both here instead of up at Noah's house, because?"

"You're right." Noah looked at his cousin. "She sure is 'spicious. Just like a teacher."

"Because?" Kit repeated, amused in spite of herself at the comparison to someone so…well, proper. A teacher. And herself. Yeah, sure.

"Because the rule in my house is," Noah replied, "we can go as far as the corner in each direction if we're with a buddy. Today Alex and I are buddies, and your house comes before the corner."

"Now can we help you?" Alex held up her wrist where an old Swiss Army watch dangled. "We'll keep track of time. Promise."

Promises. Having been given so few in her life, Kit barely knew how to react to them.

She relented. "Okay." What harm could come of giving two kids a little chore to keep them occupied for less than an hour? "You can help me give the inside of the house a once-over."

"You mean clean?" Alex asked. Both cousins looked disappointed.

"It's that or skedaddle back home."

Alex turned to Noah. "Maybe we'll turn up treasure. Last time I found my Seafaring Cecil scrapbook."

"Okay," Noah agreed. "But if my ear gets to hurtin' real bad, I'll just watch."

Alex pulled Kit down so that she could whisper in her ear. "Boys can be such babies." Then she took off up the steps, Noah in tow, to the cleaning supplies Karen had loaned Kit.

"I'll be right in," Kit called after the kids disappearing into the house. "I just have to get some bug spray out of my bike pouch." She was pretty sure two kids couldn't hurt themselves in just a couple of unsupervised minutes. The house was a mere shell with a few pieces of indestructible furniture.

As she rounded the house, Stu Hardy pulled up in front.

"What does he want?" Kit muttered, hoping the kids would stay inside, hoping, if she ignored the man, he'd go away.

He didn't.

"Well, now," Stu growled as he swaggered across the yard. "If it isn't Pritchard's Neck's latest millionaire. How does it feel to be on the side of the haves for a change, Ms. Darling?"

Kit flinched. Who had started the gossip? The McCabes? "What are you talking about, Stu?"

"Your deal with Harpswell." He came to a stop too close to her. "If you don't want your business known, you shouldn't conduct it in a public restaurant."

Ah, the cups of coffee Grant and she had had at the pier café where they'd brainstormed. Never discussed money. But small-town eavesdroppers loved to expand and project. One of the reasons she'd left.

"I'm afraid your sources aren't reliable," she replied rummaging in the Harley's side pouch for the bug bomb she'd purchased at Branson's.

"Are you telling me you didn't sign a franchise deal with Grant Harpswell?"

"I'm telling you it's none of your business." She brushed past him. "I have a house to clean."

"Well, that's why I'm here." Stu leered at her. "Inspection."

"Today's the twelfth. I have until the thirtieth."

"But with all that newfound money burning a hole in your pocket, you might figure you could skip out on old Stu."

"Why would I do that?"

He shrugged. "Because you're a Darling."

The jerk. Trying hard not to lose her cool and not to draw the kids' attention outside, she walked toward the front of the house without responding.

Stu grabbed her wrist and spun her around with force. "Not so fast."

"Let go," she warned.

"If you have money now, you can pay me for those months Babe didn't. In cash, that is. We worked out a little IOU system…in trade." He tightened his grip on Kit's wrist. "I'd appreciate the money now."

With her free hand, Kit dug into her jeans pocket to come up with a business card. She shoved it at Stu. "Have your lawyer call mine." She actually had a lawyer as of Friday—at Frederica's insistence—because of her contract with Grant.

"A lawyer. Aren't we high and mighty all of a sudden." Painfully tightening his grip on her wrist, he glanced at the card. "Roger Tarquin. Can't say as I know him."

"You wouldn't," Kit snarled. "He's a decent sort."

"I would say, Kitten, that little bit of smart mouth is uncalled for." His face a cruel mask, he pulled her up against him. "I think I need to teach you a lesson."

Having honed far too many street smarts, Kit didn't pause to think. Fueled by outrage and adrenaline, she brought her knee up in a vicious jab to the bully's groin.

Bellowing, he went down.

"What's goin' on?" Alex appeared in the doorway, Noah at her side. "What happened to Mr. Hardy?"

"My cell phone's by the door! Call 9-1-1! Tell them to send the police!" Kit barked, placing her booted foot squarely in the middle of Hardy's chest and aiming bug spray at his face. "Don't move," she growled in warning at her would-be attacker.

"But what happened?" Alex wailed, distress written all over her tiny features.

"Just call the police!"

"I'll bring you the phone."

"No! Stay on the porch. Both of you." Kit didn't want the children any closer to this mess than need be. She'd rather they were in the house, but she couldn't let Hardy up. "Make the call, Alex. 9-1-1. I need the police. Forty-four Leeward Lane."

"You bitch." Stu's eyes flashed pure, unadulterated menace, but with the bug spray in his face and his hands busy holding his groin, he lay subdued. For now.

"9-1-1? This is Alex McCabe." Alex's reedy voice wobbled, yet hung in there as she clutched the cell phone. "I need the police quick—forty-four Leeward Lane. Down the street from my aunt and uncle's house." She paused, listening. "Yeah… yeah." Then she hung up. "They're comin', Kit, but I don't understand."

"You don't have to understand, sweetie. Not right now. You and Noah go back in the house. I'll call you when you can come out."

"But—"

"Alex, I need you to go inside. Trust me on this." She had no right to ask for this little girl's trust. But didn't want two children to see this. Two children she'd put in harm's way just by being herself. A Darling. A target in this town.

She had to move on.

WORRIED ABOUT her son's ear infection, Emily stepped out on the front steps to call Noah and Alex. Brad was ready to take Noah to the doctor's and would drop Alex off at the lobster pound first.

"Noah! Alex!" she called as a police car sped down the street, blue light flashing. Her heartbeat did an extra flip. Where were those kids? At eight years old, they should be allowed some independence, but she was never wholly at ease unless her brood was within calling range. Even better if she could see them.

"Noah! Alex! Time to leave!"

The police car stopped down the street in front of Babe Darling's house. What now? A few neighbors stood on the sidewalk.

"Noah—"

Oh my God! A police incident would be a magnet for two kids. What if they'd run down there to investigate? Although she didn't see the kids standing with the others, Emily raced down the front steps as Brad poked his head out the door.

"Emily, take it easy," he called. "There's plenty of time."

"Stay with the baby. I'll get Noah and Alex," she squeaked.

She tried to stay calm, although the muscles in her throat had constricted, leaving her breathless. She tried to walk slowly, hoping Noah and Alex, in one of their endless games of hide-and-seek, would pop out of the neighbors' bushes. Hoping she could then deflect their curiosity about what the police might be doing down at the Darling house.

"Noah! Alex!" As she quickened her pace, Emily could see Babe's front yard, could see Police Officer Ken Nadick separating Kit from Stu Hardy, of all people. Emily didn't like Stu. He was too coarse for her taste, but he was one of the town's leading businessmen. People overlooked a lot when you were successful. She knew he was Babe's landlord, had even called him a couple times when Babe had really let the property grow weedy, casting a blight on the otherwise tidy neighborhood. But what could he or Kit have done to involve the police?

As angry voices crackled, the small group of spectators kept a wary distance. Just what this street needed. Noise and notoriety.

"What kind of charges are you talking about?" Ken asked, doubt evident in his voice.

"How about assault?" Kit snapped. "Or harassment. Or stalking." Waving her arms in the air, she seemed beside herself, her tough veneer worn thin.

"Stalking?" Stu howled, trying unsuccessfully to get to Kit through Ken. "I wouldn't have to stalk the likes of you. You know me, Ken. And you know her. A slut just like her mother."

"Keep it down, you two. We need to take this

to the station house." Ken eyed the spectators. "As soon as someone volunteers to get the kids home."

Kids. As the word registered, Emily saw two pale little faces pressing against one of the front windows. Noah and Alex. Dear God, had those children witnessed this sordid altercation? She tore across Babe's front yard just as Penn McCabe pulled his truck to a screeching stop behind the patrol car.

"I had the police scanner on and heard my granddaughter call 9-1-1. Where is she? Where's Alex?"

"They're here!" Running on hormones and fear, Emily, now sobbing, bounded up the porch steps, then burst through the front doorway. "Are you hurt?"

"We're okay, Mom," Noah assured her. "Alex called the police for Kit."

Penn stormed through the doorway, and Alex flung herself into his arms. "Don't be mad, Pop Pop. We were just helping Kit."

"We'll talk in a minute, sugar." He held out his hand to Emily. "Let's get these kids out of here. Do you need me to carry Noah, too?"

"No!" Emily hugged her son to her as if she'd never let him go. What had gone on here? What had the children seen? And how was it Kit Darling always seemed to trail trouble in her wake?

A second patrol car had pulled up, and that officer was putting Stu in one car, then Kit in the other as Ken Nadick made his way up onto the porch.

Penn pushed open the screen door, then held it for Emily to leave. "Do what you have to do, Ken. We're taking the youngsters home."

"Penn. Emily." Ken's face was grim. "I have to question them first. I need to know what they saw."

A startling fierceness took hold of Emily. "You need to have your head examined, Ken, if you think I'm going to let my son relive this." Carrying Noah, she brushed past the police officer and headed for Penn's truck.

She had to walk by the patrol car Kit sat in. Truculent and unrepentant. Bold as brass. And, for whatever reason, a pied piper to children. Anger overcoming her, Emily leaned low next to the window. "You haven't the sense your mother had," she said without thinking. "And she had none."

Not waiting for Kit's reaction, she followed Penn to his pickup. As he opened the passenger door for her, Alex piped up. "I didn't see anything, Pop Pop. Honest. I was sweeping."

"I saw, Mama," Noah whispered in Emily's ear. "My ear hurt. I was just sittin' by the window. Lookin' out. I saw Mr. Hardy. He was being mean to Kit. Real mean."

"Hush!" Emily commanded. "I'm sure you didn't see anything that would help the police."

Noah leaned his head against her shoulder as she slid into Penn's truck. "My ear still hurts."

"It's going to be all right, sweetheart. Daddy's

going to take you to the doctor's. Going to get some medicine to make you feel super in no time. I'll have ice cream waiting when you come home. Would you like that?"

"Yes'm."

"Now, don't you worry about what happened here. It's adult business, and the adults will have to straighten it out. Not you."

Noah snuggled closer.

Penn got in the truck as the police cruisers drove off with Stu and Kit. As if she were as much to blame as him, despite her protestations. If the police didn't believe her, who else could? Would Sean? She hated to think someone could pull the wool over an otherwise strong and perceptive man. What if the police charged Kit as a public nuisance and told her to leave town? It could happen. How would Alex feel, as tender as she was beneath that tough exterior?

Emily clutched her son. Kit leaving town might be painful for Alex and Sean, but it might be the best thing for them in the long run. You had to be able to trust people. Count on them. She was afraid all Kit could be counted on for was to break hearts.

CHAPTER THIRTEEN

SHE WAS SCARED they were going to keep her from ever seeing Kit again.

Huddled on the back staircase, trying not to be seen or heard, Alex listened to the angry voices coming from the kitchen below. Why were adults always getting so bent out of shape?

It was hard to hear exactly what people were saying because everyone was talking at once. Real loud. About what happened at Kit's this morning. But Alex had caught the gist. Uncle Brad was there on his own. He was mad 'cause he said Kit kept upsetting Aunt Emily. And then Aunt Mariah had jumped into the argument with some really bad names she'd called Kit until Dad made her stop. He said Kit was a good person, trying to clean up an ugly mess with no help from anyone in town. Yay, Dad!

Aunt Chessie had tried to stand up for Kit, saying she liked meeting her and thought she was a really creative person. But Mariah tried to make

Aunt Chessie think she couldn't know what she was talking about 'cause she and Uncle Nick were new back in town.

Pop Pop didn't want Dad to call the police to speak up for Kit. Didn't want him to say that Mr. Hardy had bothered Kit before. Pop Pop said McCabes should keep their noses out of other people's business, but Alex didn't think that was right when not helping Kit might force her to leave town. Besides, none of the family were keeping their noses out of Dad's and Alex's business.

As tears stung Alex's eyes, her visiting thirteen-year-old cousin, Gabriella, quietly slipped onto the step next to her. "You okay?" she whispered, putting her arm around Alex.

No, she was not okay, but Alex couldn't find words to say it. Instead, she leaned into Gabriella and did something she hated doing because it was only something sissies did. She cried.

And Gabriella let her. Didn't call her a baby. Didn't tell her to be quiet 'cause she'd disturb the adults. Instead, she said what Alex was feeling. "Adults are too weird."

Then she pulled a couple sour balls from who knew where and offered Alex one. "C'mon. Let's go upstairs. I got a new CD we can listen to. Reckless Graveyard Diggers. We'll turn it up real loud. If the adults can hear it over their fighting, it'll

drive 'em bonkers." She smiled. "In a good way.
It'll distract 'em."

Alex followed her cousin up the stairs. The
thought of driving the adults bonkers soothed her.
They'd been driving her bonkers for a week now,
and turnaround was fair play.

SEAN HAD HAD ENOUGH interference where Kit was
concerned. He grabbed his cell phone and headed
for the barn, leaving his family to bicker on their
own. Perhaps, without him as catalyst, they'd run
out of steam. But he doubted it.

Standing in the barn's open doorway in front of
a pile of broken lobster traps, he punched in the
number for the Public Safety Center and asked to
speak to Ken Nadick.

"Ken. Sean McCabe. I wanted to fill you in on
a couple other incidents involving Kit Darling and
Stu Hardy."

"Did you witness anything today?"

"No, but I heard you took in both Stu and Kit…
Ms. Darling."

"Had to," Nadick replied. "The kids were the
only real witnesses, and they said they saw nothing. It became a case of he-said-she-said."

"Are you still holding them?"

"No. They each lawyered up. We let them
both go."

"Both?"

"Sean, you and I know Stu. He can be rough around the edges, but he's a citizen. Big landowner. Chamber of commerce. Elks—"

"But he's been harassing Kit. I've witnessed it twice before today, and I'll swear to it. Once in Branson's. Once on her property—"

"Stu's property," Nadick interjected.

"There must be laws that protect renters."

"Kit isn't even the renter. Her mother is, and her mother's left the state."

"And Kit's trying to clean up the property before turning over the key."

"Sean, take a friend's advice, and stop worrying about Kit. Her lawyer's Roger Tarquin, a shrewd son of a gun who usually handles Portland's upper crust. How Kit found him is anyone's guess. Strange bedfellows, as they say. Anyhoo, Tarquin was talking restraining order, so my thought is it's not your battle to fight."

Sean clenched his teeth. It didn't appear Ken was going to throw much police support behind a Darling cause. "You can't just let Stu get away with this—"

He stopped short as Kit guided her Harley up the McCabes' driveway and cut the motor right in front of him.

"I have to go, Ken. But I'm serious about swearing to those other two incidents." He hung up before the officer could respond.

Kit didn't bother with formalities. "How's Alex?"

"She's okay. How are you?" He hoped against hope that this last unpleasant incident hadn't soured her on the town once and for all.

"I've been better. And I've been worse. Stu Hardy's a bully, but bullies can be made to back down. He'll understand the language Roger Tarquin speaks."

"I'm glad to see you're letting a lawyer handle it."

Kit shrugged. "Hardy's not worth my time."

"Still, it seems he's got a mean streak. You've brought him up short. Embarrassed him. If he comes within a mile of you, I—"

She held up her hand to stop him. "It's under control, but…thanks for the offer."

She was thanking him? Kit was thanking him for an offer of help she would have sneered at a week ago? Would wonders never cease? In spite of the day's serious events, he grinned.

And she smiled back. Another miracle. But all too quickly the smile dissipated. "I just dropped by to make sure Alex wasn't traumatized," she said softly, her gray eyes clouded with concern. "I'm really sorry, Sean. I wouldn't hurt Alex for the world."

"I know you wouldn't."

"But what she saw—"

"I explained to her that you were standing up for yourself."

"Then you had to explain—at least in part—about Stu and what he was doing."

"Yes."

"You must hate me for bringing such ugliness into your daughter's life."

"I could never hate you, Kit." On the contrary, he was beginning to feel so deeply for her that his protective instincts went out to her as much as his family. "Besides, you may have taught Alex a valuable lesson."

"How could that be?"

"By disabling Stu, by pressing charges, you showed her females don't need to think they're powerless."

Her eyes widened in surprise.

Loud voices erupted from the open windows of the main house. It seemed his family wasn't finished trying to run his life by committee.

Kit appeared to understand the situation immediately. "I never wanted to get any of your family involved, but…"

"But what?" When he moved to take her hand, she shifted her weight on the cycle, crossed her arms and put her hands tightly under them.

She didn't speak, although the troubled look on

her face said she wrestled with something. Frederica had said Kit carried a secret, and, in carrying it, was willing to sacrifice her happiness for his. So how did he make a woman prickly and suspicious by nature feel safe enough to open up?

"Kit—" he motioned toward the opened windows and the raised voices "—don't let my family get to you. We're just like almost any other family. Loud. Opinionated. Bossy. But that's because we love each other. We trust each other enough to be honest, painful as that is sometimes."

When he stepped forward to take her hands, this time she let him. Her fingers felt small, warm and fragile.

"I told you once that my life is my own," he went on, trying to bring her into that life, into the part that might win her trust. "I make my own decisions. My family may talk a good show, but none of them get to make my decisions for me. Especially not any decisions I choose to make about you. About us."

She started a little at the word *us,* but she didn't withdraw.

"My family's in there—" he nodded at the house "—arguing in circles about something they have no control over." He placed her small hand on his chest, over his heart. "I'm here. And I'm the only one who has control over me. Over my life."

He grinned. "Well, except for Alex, but she and I are in total agreement where you're concerned."

Kit swallowed hard before looking directly at him. "You know, I came to tell you goodbye," she said, her words almost inaudible. "But I can't quite bring myself to do it."

He exhaled sharply and discovered he'd been holding his breath. His heart beat more rapidly. "Then don't."

"So, what do I do instead?"

"Have dinner with me tomorrow night. Let's start over. With a date. A real date."

A hint of mischief returned to her eyes. "You're not afraid that's a bit bourgeois?"

"The only thing I'm afraid of is losing you. Again. Before we give what's between us a chance."

She seemed to take his words and weigh them carefully. "A date," she breathed at last. "Okay."

Sean couldn't imagine three better words in the English language. "I'll pick you up at Frederica's. Tomorrow night at seven."

"I'll be ready," she said, apparently surprised at her own acquiescence. Withdrawing her hands from his, she started the Harley and wheeled down the driveway before he could kiss her. Which he desperately wanted to do. To seal their agreement. To share some of his happiness.

Instead, he returned to the house and his argumentative family. A hush fell over the kitchen as he entered. He used the moment to make his announcement.

"I'm seeing Kit. Officially," he declared. "Get used to it."

Then he took the back stairs two at a time to tell his daughter the good news.

SO AS NOT TO THINK about the date she'd just agreed to, Kit pulled the Harley in front of Branson's store and tried to think about how she should handle her mother's request for money to get home.

Putting on her game face, she squared her shoulders and strode into the store. Just let someone confront her about her actions against Stu Hardy. She now had money and means, and she had what the old salts called gumption. She didn't need to defer to anyone in this town.

As usual, several customers watched her progress down the aisles to the office in the back of the store where she planned to send a fax. She kept her eyes straight ahead, only patting her jeans pocket to make sure she had Babe's fax. She still didn't have any idea how she was going to respond.

Did there ever come a point when a child had to cut a parent off? Did that make the child an ungrateful wretch or just smart?

Kit's decision now also involved the appearance of Emily McCabe. Babe's daughter. Kit's sister. Kit felt certain Emily didn't know about Babe. Call it gut instinct. Her scrapbooks alone showed Emily felt herself a Chesterton through and through. But did Babe know about Emily? Babe had moved here from Vermont twenty-four years ago and had never left. Had she continued searching for her daughter? She wasn't a woman to exert herself much beyond her love life. Emily had moved here from Portland nine years ago, right after high school. Had Babe discovered the newcomer's identity? Had she tried to reveal herself to Emily and been rebuffed? Was that why Emily was so cool and aloof toward Kit? So many questions.

Kit didn't delude herself into thinking Emily might want a kid sister's protection. Especially not a kid sister with Darling for a last name. Emily had the double protection of Chestertons and McCabes to counter any overt move Babe might make. Might have made. But what if neither of them knew the mother-daughter connection? Wasn't that little secret a ticking time bomb?

Kit never asked for the whole sisterhood scenario. Didn't want it now, especially considering the sister was Emily. But deep, deep, deep inside she felt the right thing to do would be to keep Babe from inflicting any more harm.

"May I help you?"

Startled, Kit found herself in front of a counter where a pretty blonde, about thirty, stood. Reaching into her pocket, Kit said, "I received this fax and would like to respond."

The blonde took the fax and read it, apparently unruffled by Babe's signature or the reference to Ed Crenshaw. "Oh, sure. You can wire money from here."

"I don't want to wire money. I want to fax a reply. Will she get it, do you think?"

"Believe me, if she's expecting money, she'll be checking regularly. She'll get your fax." The woman cocked one eyebrow. "She won't be happy, but she'll get it."

Kit didn't need any editorializing. She grabbed a pen and a fax form from the counter and wrote:

Babe—I took care of the house and your debts. There's no money left over to send you. I'll be leaving town, so there's nothing left for you here. In fact, Stu Hardy says he can make plenty of trouble for you if you return. Ditto, Millicent Crenshaw. Ditto, your creditors. Stay where you are. Get a job. Start over—Kit.

Not knowing how to make the message any stronger—she'd fudged the plenty-of-trouble part, although she could imagine it coming true—she handed the paper to the clerk.

"That'll be three dollars," the woman said, glancing at the message as she put it through the fax machine.

Kit lay three ones on the counter, then turned to leave.

"Are you the woman who slapped a restraining order on Stu?"

The words made Kit stop in her tracks, but she didn't turn to look back. "I don't see where it's any of your business."

"It is," the woman insisted, "in a roundabout way."

Kit turned to stare into blue eyes that held no contempt. Only regret. "What do you mean?"

"I wish I had your guts. So do a lot of women in this town who've been on the unwanted end of Stu's advances. He's a pig. A coward who's careful to hide his true colors from most of the guys or people he thinks can be useful. You see, I'm single with no family in town. Kind of like you. Easy prey. Stu won't go after women who have a strong support system. It's time someone stood up for us." She handed the fax back to Kit. "Here, keep this as your receipt."

"Sure." Kit took the paper, then folded it with Babe's message. "Thanks."

"No problem." The woman smiled before turning to a messy stack of files.

Kit left the store a little undone by the unexpected show of support.

Sitting on her motorcycle in the parking lot, she felt a jolt of realization. It wasn't the rejection in her hometown that was the challenge. It was the prospect of acceptance. This woman's just now. Grant's. Frederica's. Alex's. Sean's. She could battle rejection. She had her entire life. She'd perfected her psychological defenses. But acceptance scared the hell out of her.

She couldn't face a date with Sean tomorrow night. She needed to keep her edge and focus on the solitary life she'd successfully carved out for herself.

She'd told Babe to stay away and start over. Well, Kit needed to follow her own advice. Actually, she was one step ahead of the game. She had a job. A great job that had just taken a turn for the better. A job that didn't have to involve this town or these people and their tricky acceptance. Didn't have to involve Sean and his openness and his sexy grin and his kisses. And his terrific kid. Accepting what he offered was a siren's song indeed.

She needed to break the date.

She turned the Harley back in the direction of the McCabe household.

Temptation didn't open the front door at Sean's. Chessie McCabe did. "Kit! What a pleasant surprise!" She stepped back in welcome. "Come in, come in."

Kit would have preferred Emily or Mariah to answer the door. At this moment, she needed a good dose of cold shoulder to implement her decision.

"Is Sean here?" she asked, hoping he was right around the corner and she could make this short and sweet. In the doorway. Away from family.

Instead, Chessie took her by the hand to lead her toward the sound of laughter and easy banter, very different from the argument she'd heard through the window earlier. Were family dynamics so quick to change? Kit was clueless where families were concerned.

"I really wanted to talk more about your work," Chessie said. "It's so nice to meet a fellow artist. A kindred spirit."

Kit swallowed hard. Chessie's quick welcome and talk of kindred spirits didn't encourage Kit to sever ties.

Neither did the scene in the kitchen.

There was no sign of Sean's father, his sister or brothers Brad and Jonas. Sean, Alex, Nick and his daughters, Gabriella and Isabel, sat around the kitchen table spread with a Monopoly game in wild session. The bartering was heated, the accusations affectionate, while the thrill of victory and the agony of defeat hung palpable in the air. An empty chair indicated that Chessie had been playing as well.

"Kit!" Sean looked up, surprise and pleasure on his rugged features. "You came back—join us."

"Yeah!" Alex seconded. She waved a fistful of play money. "It's Monopoly, and I'm winning!"

"You can take her place," Gabriella offered, giving her cousin a playful nudge. "It's past her bedtime."

"Is not!" Alex crowed. "You're just mad 'cause I'm eight and I'm beating you."

"Alex is the Donald Trump of Monopoly," Chessie added.

"If you want a chance to beat her at any game," Nick interjected, "challenge her to cribbage. Then, and only then, will you have a fifty-fifty chance of winning."

"She's lucky," Isabel declared.

"Am not." Alex tapped her forehead. "I'm crafty. Dad says so."

Kit was dumbfounded by the way this branch of Sean's family so easily enveloped her. Maybe it was because Nick and Chessie were eight years older than Scan and were long gone from Pritchard's Neck before Kit hit high school.

Nick reached around behind him to snag an extra chair. "Join us. Then you can have a say in where Sean takes you on your date tomorrow night." He grinned that same boyish way Sean did.

"Everybody else has put in their two cents' worth. Since you're actually involved, you might as well have a vote, too."

Kit stood stock-still, ignoring the proffered chair. Sean had told his family about their date? The date she'd come to break?

"I have to say," Chessie mused, still standing at her side, "the idea that got the most votes was Alex's. She thinks her dad needs to dress up in mud and ostrich feathers and dance and sing for you on Frederica Harpswell's lawn."

Alex smiled at Kit. "Like the Wodabe!"

"Yeah, Uncle Sean," Gabriella added impishly, "you could sell tickets to that."

Seemingly unfazed by the teasing, Sean pulled the extra chair close to his own. He cast a hot glance at Kit and patted the seat. "Join us," he reiterated. "I'd be interested to hear your ideas on the first-date subject."

He wasn't just unfazed by his family's attention. He basked in it. And by offering her a chair right by his side, he was offering to share the warmth with her. Kit could actually see herself a part of the family.

She tried to remember why she was here. She needed to break tomorrow's date and end the possibility of any more involvement with this far too appealing man.

But Chessie thwarted Kit's resolve by gently

propelling her to the chair next to Sean. She sat, but didn't trust herself to speak.

As naturally as if they were a couple, Sean slipped his arm around her shoulders, causing her pulse to pick up. "So," he said, his voice an intimate rumble in her ear, "where do you think we should go tomorrow?"

Oh, she was in way over her head.

"I think it should be somewhere romantic," offered dreamy-eyed Isabel. "A moonlit boat ride."

Alex wrinkled her nose. "Dad's boat smells like bait."

"Hey!" Gabriella came to life. "I saw an ad in *The Tourist News* for balloon rides over in Wells."

"Girls, girls," Chessie interjected with a sly look at Sean. "You have to realize Uncle Sean has his work cut out for him. Kit is a woman who has traveled the world. As Seafaring Cecil, she's lived romance."

"So, what are you saying, Chess?" Sean ran his fingers down Kit's arm, trailing heat and expectation in their wake. "I'm boring?"

Chessie shared a wink with Kit. "All I'm saying is that a guy would have to dig deep to determine what could woo such a woman."

Nick rolled his eyes. "Chessie's developed this thing about wooing."

"Not a thing, husband of mine." Chessie bristled just the slightest. "A firm conviction that wooing keeps the relationship alive. Before and after marriage."

"So how shall I woo you?" Sean asked Kit, his words low enough that she knew he meant them for her alone.

"You can't ask her," Chessie insisted, unabashedly eavesdropping. "Asking negates the essence of wooing. You have to understand—"

"I understand—" grinning, Sean rose, pulling Kit with him "—that wooing involves more privacy than I'm going to get in this kitchen. If you'll excuse us…" He handed his Monopoly money to Gabriella who had very little of her own remaining. "Consider us partners, kiddo."

As he escorted Kit to the front door, Alex called after them, "K-i-s-s-i-n-g's always good, Dad!"

He chuckled, and the throaty sound made Kit warm all over. "Finally, an idea I can get behind," he murmured.

As soon as they were out of sight and before she could decline their date, he pulled her against him and captured her mouth with his.

What she could not get over—when her thoughts returned to earth—was how right it felt in Sean's arms. Right, despite all the arguments that pointed out how wrong they were for each other.

Sean trailed kisses over her cheek. Nuzzled her

ear. Made her knees weak and her blood sing. "I wanted to kiss you back in the barn," he whispered huskily. "When you first agreed to go out with me. But you ran away." He slid his fingers up her neck and into her hair. "What made you come back?"

His touch made her woozy. She couldn't bring herself to say, "I came back to tell you I can't see you again."

Instead, she murmured, "This. I came back for this." And wondered if she hadn't spoken the absolute truth.

CHAPTER FOURTEEN

THE FOLLOWING NIGHT, ringing Frederica's doorbell at seven sharp, Sean felt as nervous as a teenager about to pick up his prom date. Electricity seemed to dance in the air as Kit stepped out on the veranda.

She wore a sleek vintage dress of pale gray silk that caressed the curves of her body. Devoid of makeup, her skin fairly glowed. Her hair was softer than usual, more tousled than spiky, the color muted. On her feet were beaded evening sandals.

Almost shyly, she smiled, then twirled in front of him. "Frederica and I raided her attic."

"Wow."

"I take it you approve, Mr. McCabe."

"Kit Darling, you don't need anyone's approval. All by yourself, you're a force to be reckoned with."

She blushed. "So, where are we going?"

"A little out-of-the-way place I know." He grinned as he put his hand on the small of her back and guided her to his truck.

The truck. A more romantic guy would have hired a limo or a horse-drawn carriage—as strongly suggested by Alex, Gabriella and Isabel—or, at the very least, borrowed his brother Nick's new sedan. But in his late-night confab with his sister-in-law Chessie, Sean had decided he needed to be himself. Even Chessie agreed he shouldn't woo a woman like Kit Darling with pretension. And so he'd scrubbed his old truck, inside and out, to within an inch of its life and planned a simple yet intimate evening that would allow them to talk. To reconnect.

As he helped her into the cab of the truck, he noticed six brand-new kayaks overturned on Frederica's lawn. "What's that all about?" he asked.

"A surprise from Grant. A signing bonus. Seems he and Frederica think I should find some time to establish a side business out of Pritchard's Neck. Coastal exploration. Tours. Day trips." She looked unsure. "What do you think?"

"You know what I think." He twined his fingers through hers, then raised her hand to his lips. "I think it's a great idea."

Releasing her hand, he gently shut the passenger door. On his way around the truck to the driver's side, he eyed the colorful kayaks one more time. Of course the business was a great idea. Anything that kept Kit here. But…those expensive kayaks brought home yet another difference between Kit and himself.

For him, money was a constant concern, his income dependent on weather, tides and a crop he had no control over. For Kit, money seemed unimportant. Easy come, easy go. While he struggled to stay one step ahead of the game, she made no big deal about signing a contract that came with a half-dozen toy boats as a bonus.

His provider instinct took a hit.

But the look of eager anticipation Kit gave him as he slid behind the wheel dissolved some of his misgivings. She seemed glad to be with him. Not with Grant Harpswell in his Ferrari, but with Sean McCabe in his battered but squeaky-clean truck.

"I thought," she said, "you and Alex and I could take three of the kayaks out on their maiden voyage. Tomorrow. After you finish hauling traps. After school hours, so that Alex's principal can't accuse her of wasting time."

"I'd like that." He took a deep breath and let go a little more of his self-doubt.

They drove in silence to the nearly finished lobster pound, where he parked in front, fielding a quizzical look from Kit. As he jumped out of the truck to open Kit's door, he hoped Chessie's and his idea worked. And that, in trying to keep things simple, he wouldn't look like some bumbling rube.

He didn't want to impress Kit. He wanted her to feel at ease. Cared for. On his home turf.

"Am I getting a tour?" Mischievous light danced in her gray eyes. "You heard I came into some money. This must be an investors recruitment banquet."

"You, madam, may keep your money. There'll be no discussion of business. Tonight is strictly personal."

To emphasize his point, he led her, not through the pound—of which he was inordinately proud—but along the outside walkway that led to the wharf. Ah, yes, his co-conspirator Chessie had worked her magic. As had Mother Nature.

"Oh, Sean!" Kit gasped softly.

The sun hung low over the horizon, casting the harbor in delicate pinks. The water lapping gently at the pylons created a counterpoint to the soft music coming from the radio in his office. The air was redolent with a salt tang mixed with the heady sweetness of freshly cut and planed lumber. Chessie had strung tiny white lights along the back of the building and had set a table for two in the middle of the wharf. Linen. China. Crystal. Flowers. Candlelight from a hurricane lamp. His sister-in-law had taken his vision and turned it into reality. And it seemed to meet Kit's approval.

He held a chair out for her. Inhaled the fresh

scent of her hair as she sat. Urged himself to get through dinner before he took her in his arms. "I'm afraid the butler has taken the night off. I'll be right back."

In his office mini-fridge, he found the prepared plates of lobster salad, the chilled white wine. A baguette of crusty French bread lay wrapped in a linen napkin on a tray. He carried everything back out to Kit as an offering. This was the fruit of his labor. This was what he did. This was who he was. What she saw would be what she got. Anything he might become in the future…well, that was up to her.

Kit was staring out into the harbor at the *Alexandra* tugging gently at her mooring. When she looked at him, her eyes were moist.

"Are you okay?" he asked, placing the food before her, filling their wineglasses.

"This is beautiful," she sighed, fingering the stem of her glass. "I love my life, but…if I ever had a home, it would look just like this. Right here."

He knew it had taken a great deal of courage for her to say that.

Sitting across from her, he slid his hand over the table to cover hers. "I love my life, too, but sometimes I get wanderlust so intense it hurts."

"It can be lonely," she replied with a wistful smile. "And here you have Alex. A big family."

"You can be lonely surrounded by people."

Her eyes widened. "Yes. I always felt lonely with my mother."

"Ah, Kit." He turned her hand palm up, caressed the soft pad at the base of her thumb. "It's a shame we get to pick our friends, our business associates, but family…sometimes family's like Russian roulette."

With her free hand she grasped his wrist. "I have to tell you what I've done. I don't know if it makes me a bad person or not."

"You're not bad, Kit. Never were. Never will be. A handful, maybe, but not bad."

She licked her lips. "Babe sent a fax. Sunday. Asking me to send money. Seems she and Ed have parted ways. She wants to come back to Pritchard's Neck."

Sean flinched. Was this the burdensome secret Frederica had alluded to? Babe would make life in this town intolerable for Kit.

"What did you do?"

"I sent her a return fax. Told her I wouldn't be sending a cent. Told her to stay away and start over." Tears rose in her eyes. "I've quit playing parent to my mother, but…was it responsible, or was I just getting back at her?"

"You exercised tough love," he assured her. "You couldn't let your mother pull you down. It doesn't make you an uncaring person. I know otherwise." He smiled. "So does Alex. Frederica. Even my sister-in-law Chessie."

"It's easy with you guys." She swiped at her eyes. "You're the greatest."

"You had to stop rescuing your mother—" he used his thumb to wipe away the last of the moisture at the corners of her eyes "—and concentrate on your own life. To the fullest."

Sean's advice gave him pause. He wanted what was best for her. He really did. But was the best for her best for him? For Alex? If Kit and he were to have a future, would it smother her? For Kit to be a wife and mother, would she have to cut back her career? Moreover, if she chose to move on, he didn't know if he'd have the strength to say goodbye.

"I want to believe you," she replied. Kit looked into Sean's eyes and admitted to herself that what he thought of her, of her actions, mattered.

Sean was an estimable man.

And tonight he was being so kind. So thoughtful. And so sexy. The harborside setting he'd concocted was lovely. It was clear he was, to use his sister-in-law's term, wooing her. That frightened Kit a little.

Sean gently squeezed her hand. "Is something wrong?"

"No." She shook her head, reassured by his touch. "No. Quite the contrary." She returned the pressure of his hand. "I'm enjoying the moment."

They ate lobster and drank wine and watched the sun set, and never once stopped holding hands. It was as if they both recognized the fragility of their situation.

"You talked to your sister-in-law about me?" she asked tentatively.

"Sure. Chessie's easy to talk to. And right from the start, she liked you. Besides, you didn't think a guy collecting dust could pull this off without a little help?" He smiled as he indicated the elegant table, the lights.

It pleased Kit that this big, strong, competent man had asked for help. For her.

"I managed the lobster and the wine," he continued. "But dessert is pure Chessie. Some mocha-cheesecake concoction that she calls her signature creation. She only makes it for family functions. I had to bribe her big time to make it for us. Assured her you…that you were worth it."

Kit felt heat creep into her cheeks and rose from her seat to redirect Sean's attention. "Then let's bring out this masterpiece," she said, clearing their plates.

"Sit." He took the plates from her. "You're the guest."

"But I want to see inside the pound."

"Not romantic." He cocked one eyebrow in warning, but she didn't pay attention.

As he disappeared through the back doorway, she followed him and found herself in an office complete with built-in cabinetry and furniture, as spare and shipshape as the interior of a boat. Although the pound hadn't opened for business yet, the office looked used. Lived in, even. The desk was a mess. Alex's drawings nearly covered the walls and, on a built-in bunk along one wall, it appeared his daughter had made a nest of a thick quilt and a couple dozen books.

"The maid's day off, too?" she teased.

"I told you it wasn't romantic." He pulled a luscious-looking cheesecake from the fridge.

"But that is!" She indicated the dessert. "And it screams picnic." She grabbed the quilt from the bunk. "There's a limit to sitting at tables in chairs, and I think I've reached it. Follow me."

She liked the desire that flickered in his eyes.

On the wharf again, she spread the quilt away from the table and chairs, under the darkening sky. The strings of tiny white lights suddenly went out. Surprised, she looked up to see Sean standing in the doorway, holding two plates of cheesecake.

"The stars aren't as bright with the lights on." Crossing the wharf, he blew out the candle on the table, as well. "And you have to see the stars."

He sat next to her on the quilt. Very close. She found his bulk and his warmth reassuring and exciting at the same time. A soft breeze caressed her, and she reminded herself to slow down. Enjoy the moment. Suspend any expectations beyond right now.

He set one plate on the wharf. From the other, he cut a piece of cheesecake, then lifted the fork to her mouth. "Try this. It will have you eating from my hand."

"If I try it, won't I be eating from your hand?"

"You're too clever by half, Kit Darling." He chuckled.

She accepted the bite of cheesecake he offered, and its wonderful sweetness slid across her tongue. Sean was right. The dessert was special—family tradition and love and a gift all rolled into one. "Thank you," she said. "For everything."

He put down the plate, and pulled her close. He kissed her mouth and her nose and her eyes and her hair. She ran her fingers over his face, felt his warmth and his intent. Tried to imprint his features by touch in case tomorrow he was a memory.

He lay back on the quilt, pulling her to his side. "Look," he said softly, pointing skyward. "Venus."

The planet was the brightest object in the moonless sky, a sky so velvety that Kit felt as if she were wrapped in a protective indigo cocoon. Just herself and this man who seemed to want her despite all the obvious obstacles. Tonight she wanted to play with him under the stars.

"There's Orion," he continued. "Alex's favorite. Mine's the Little Dipper. A sailor's constellation." He paused. "We tried to get Jilian interested, but she said all she saw were stars. She could never see the stories or the mystery."

"Do you miss her?" Kit realized that, except for the one time in the hospital parking lot, Sean hadn't talked about his wife.

He didn't answer right away, lay very still beside her, and Kit wondered if the reminder had hurt him.

"I've never told anyone this," he began, his voice halting. "I still grieve. But not in the way people expect. My grief is…that I didn't love Jilian the way she deserved before she died."

Beside him, Kit was stunned. "But you stood by her," she countered. "You married her. You had a daughter together."

"Our relationship went from teenage exploration to family responsibility in a heartbeat. Skipping too many stages in between."

"Are you saying you never had feelings for her?" Kit didn't understand. "You seemed like the perfect couple in high school."

"Sure, I had feelings for her. But there's a big difference between chemistry and love. I think the chemistry blinded us."

"And who you are in high school is a far cry from who you might become at, say, twenty-five or even twenty-one."

"Exactly. But being married at eighteen made me feel as if I had to grow up. Right then. That any changes were a done deal. Behind me. At first, I felt enormous resentment. I felt trapped. Didn't see that it was my own doing as much as Jilian's. God, we were young. And then Alex came. I loved her. Fiercely. And because I loved her, I began to love her mother. But Jilian died before…."

Kit placed her hand on his chest. "And you've felt guilty ever since."

"Yes." His response was no more than a raspy whisper, but his pain spoke volumes.

"Let it go, Sean. Let it go."

"How?"

She didn't know. Strangely, although she felt for Sean, she empathized with Jilian. It was sad not to get a full measure of love.

"I can't really say. I come from a family that excels at withholding love."

"I'm sorry. Babe was never the maternal type. But you, you're so open. You withhold nothing."

She inhaled sharply. She didn't know if she could voice this one secret.

He picked up on her reticence. "You don't agree?"

He turned so that they were both on their sides on the quilt, face-to-face, inches from each other.

"You told me something you've never told anyone before," she began. "I guess it's my turn." She cleared her throat, looked down at the first button of his shirt. "I'm a virgin. A twenty-four-year-old virgin."

He said nothing. Absolutely nothing.

Still not looking at him, she continued. "It's not from lack of opportunity. I've held on to my virginity deliberately. With a vengeance. In the face of my mother's lack of control, it's been a symbol of ultimate control for me."

He tipped her chin so that she had to look at him. "So, you've withheld love, too," he said simply.

She nodded.

He sighed. "And what did we prove?"

"Not much."

"And ended up shortchanging ourselves in the bargain."

He caressed her cheek with his fingertips. "There's something between us, Kit, that can't be denied. Are we going to stop on the brink?"

To love this man, if only for one night, couldn't be wrong.

"No. I don't want to stay closed off. Not from you."

Threading her fingers through his hair, she

pulled him into a kiss. Kissed him with passion and want and need and tomorrow-be-damned. And he returned her fervor. As his tongue met hers, as his arms wrapped tightly, possessively around her, she felt a tiny, bunched up place inside her unfurl.

The moonless night was now so dark it seemed like they were the only two on earth, on a soft quilt bed, beneath a starry canopy. For tonight, Sean was her universe.

Sean felt drenched in Kit's kiss.

He broke away only to trail a series of nips and licks down her throat. She made a soft purring sound, which he felt more than heard. Undeniably, she wanted him as much as he wanted her. Making love to Kit tonight could not be the end. It had to be a beginning.

Running his hands along her body, he felt the warmth of her skin beneath the silky dress. He tried to still his racing heart. Tried to soften his desire so that he didn't take her too suddenly, too roughly. This was her first time. He was her first. He'd tried to make her understand how much she meant to him. Now, his body needed to confirm his innermost feelings.

As he kissed her collarbone, she threaded her fingers through his hair and arched against him. He felt the warmth of her strong, lithe body as if it were part of his own. He lay his ear against her

breast and heard the thumping of her heart, an
echo of his. With his hands he explored her body,
uncharted territory. Under his touch her soft
breasts became his. Her gently sloping belly, his.
Her thighs, his. The warmth and moistness and
mystery between her legs, his. And where his
hands went his mouth and tongue and teeth followed until he was dizzy with wanting her and
having her all at the same time.

"Oh, Sean! Oh!" Her words seemed to sing in
his bloodstream.

Her hands began to explore him. She moved aside
his clothing as if she had always known him. Her
touch against his bare skin nearly drove him mad.

Without a word, they came together, both of
them moving. When he felt as if he couldn't hold
back any longer, she whispered his name fiercely
in his ear. As he felt her shudder beneath him, he
let himself go over the edge. Into the abyss, body
and soul.

Kit felt the waves wash over her. No book had ever
prepared her for this sensation of total abandonment.
Her body throbbed. Her mind reeled. She had never
felt so much a part of another human being.

How did people treat sex—lovemaking—so casually? It was a gift. And a sacrifice. And a trust.

Sean held her, kissing her hair.

With his fingertips he traced the line of her jaw.

"A penny for your thoughts." His voice was gruff and gravelly.

"I'm speechless."

Funny, but she could feel him grin in the dark. "Now there's a first."

She sighed. "One of many."

He lay on his back, pulling her with him so that his chest made a pillow for her.

A meteorite streaked across the sky. "Shooting star!" they said in unison.

"Make a wish," he urged, stroking her arm. "Out loud."

She paused before she spoke, searching for something heartfelt, something that would honor what they'd shared.

"I wish," she said at last, "that people would stop withholding love."

"I second that," he declared, pulling her to him in a kiss that was heightened by all that had come before.

Melting against him, Kit couldn't help adding one more silent wish, although she knew she was entitled to only one. She wished this night with Sean would never end.

CHAPTER FIFTEEN

"YOU HAVE THE LOOK, my dear, of a woman in love." With a twinkle in her eye, Frederica put down her book next to her fan chair as Kit, coffee cup in hand, stepped dreamily onto the veranda.

Morning had come and gone, and she'd spent the hours lying on her bed, alternately dozing and remembering. Dawn, when Sean had reluctantly dropped her off so that he could head out to work, seemed ages ago. Last night had altered the world. The sky was brighter. The ocean more magnificent. The afternoon shadows more tender. Her heart more open.

"And your preoccupation confirms my suspicions." Frederica's voice came to her as if from a great distance.

Kit smiled. "Suspicions?"

"That you are in love, dear girl." Beaming, Frederica reached out to take Kit's hand. "And I couldn't be happier for you."

Kit couldn't be happier either, but that couldn't

completely mask her skepticism. "But can you fall in love—really fall in love—in just one week?"

"I met my husband one afternoon during the war. At a tea party for American servicemen." Frederica's eyes misted with a faraway look. "Before the scones were gone, I knew he was the man with whom I wished to spend my life."

"And you were in the middle of a war. How could you be sure things would work out?"

"I couldn't. Nothing is certain. Ever. I simply took the plunge and gave him my heart." She held tightly to Kit's hand.

"Besides," Frederica added, "you've known Sean for much longer than a week."

Yes. Yes, she had. And she'd been a little bit in love with him nine years ago.

"Hello." Sean's deep voice settled over her with all the sensuality of a cashmere shawl. "Did you forget our date? The kayaks."

She turned to see him standing at the corner of the house, tall and lean and relaxed in a fresh shirt and clean jeans, watching her hungrily.

"Oh, no!" She looked at her watchless wrist. "What time is it?"

"Two-thirty." He raised an eyebrow and indicated the rumpled, oversize T-shirt she'd obviously slept in, the coffee cup in her hand. "Sleepyhead."

Grinning, he crossed the veranda and bent to

give her an uninhibited kiss. As if he didn't care that Frederica might think they were a couple. His lips were warm and smooth and dry and tasted of promises.

That buzz she felt didn't come from Karen's strong coffee.

"Where's Alex?" she asked, to see if she could put two words together.

"She and Jonas went to see Emily and the baby. I thought we could tow her kayak up the harbor. There's a little shingle beach across the street from Brad and Emily's house. We can pick her up from there."

"I'm so glad you're going to use the kayaks," Frederica interjected. "I'm sure the three of you can come up with some very creative ideas for a sideline for Kit." She smiled innocently. "A business out of Pritchard's Neck, of course."

"Of course," Sean agreed way too quickly.

Of course. "I'll be just a sec." A little unnerved, Kit rose to go change, to discontinue this conversation.

A sideline based in Pritchard's Neck, indeed, she mused, hurrying up to the guest room.

She caught herself even as her usual knee-jerk response to anything related to this seaside strip of Maine kicked in. What was so crazy about the idea? Kit had mentioned it to Alex the day they'd gone lobstering. And Alex had repeated it to Grant at the McCabe party. And Grant had run with the ball. It was a good idea, even if Kit didn't necessarily need to be the one to implement it.

But why shouldn't she? She'd kept herself solvent and Seafaring Cecil fresh by remaining open to new ideas. And staying in Pritchard's Neck, if only for a few months a year, was certainly a novel idea.

Sean loomed large as a reason for her change of heart, although the passion he engendered made her almost as skittish as the antipathy she used to feel for this place. Alex surely made her want to hang around. Who wouldn't want to associate with someone who accepted you immediately, unconditionally? And then there was Frederica. Frederica listened to her. Comforted her. Encouraged her. As a real parent might.

A surrogate parent, a friend, a lover. These were strong inducements to stay, to put down roots.

She hastened to change clothes and face all these wonderful, emerging possibilities with a newly opened mind.

When she returned to the veranda, Sean was engrossed in a phone conversation, his expression serious, his stance tense.

"Sorry." He flipped his cell phone shut. "I can't make it kayaking. Seems a yacht trying to maneuver the moorings in the harbor grazed the *Alexandra*."

"Oh, no!" Kit moved to his side. "Is it serious?"

"The harbormaster assures me it's not, but I have to get back to the pier to meet with the owner and the insurance people."

"I'll call Alex and cancel."

"No," he insisted. "Don't cancel. Alex would be heartbroken. Pick her up at the beach as we planned. I'll phone ahead from the truck to let them know you're coming alone."

Kit inhaled sharply. The idea of picking up Alex at Emily's was not pleasant. Not after the fiasco with Stu Hardy and the upset it had understandably caused the kids. "Perhaps we should just postpone until you can come."

"Believe me, Kit, there are many outings ahead for us." With a look of unabashed tenderness, he brushed an errant wisp of her hair behind her ear. "This afternoon I need you to distract Alex. If she thinks the *Alexandra*'s in trouble, she'll freak. I'll just tell her I got tied up at the pier. Hopefully, the damage is minimal and I can take care of it before explaining at supper tonight."

He brushed his lips against Kit's.

She mustered a smile as he left, but she was apprehensive about the day.

"This is getting way too complicated."

"Kit, this is life, and it's just getting interesting." Frederica patted Kit's shoulder.

As Kit hauled two lightweight kayaks over the lawn to the water, she considered her solitary career of travel and adventure—and it seemed not so much solitary anymore, as a little bit lonely. Sure, she still wanted her career, but she wanted Sean and Alex and Frederica, too. Why couldn't she have it all?

The sleek kayaks were state of the art and swift—Grant had spared no expense—and, in no time, Kit pulled up on the little rocky beach across the street from Emily's house. Emily, the woman who said Kit hadn't a lick of sense. Her sister. How could Kit separate her newfound happiness in Pritchard's Neck from Emily? She wished she didn't have to take that short walk across the street.

Perhaps Alex would be waiting outside. But Kit couldn't just take Alex without telling Emily. Alex was in her care for the afternoon. Kit had to start thinking like a responsible adult.

There was no sign of Alex. Steeling herself, she climbed Emily's front steps, then rang the doorbell.

Emily appeared behind the screen door, holding her baby. "Is there something I can do for you?" she asked, her tone icily polite.

"I'm here to pick up Alex." Kit tried to keep her voice even. "But I want to tell you I'm sorry Noah got caught up in that mess with Stu Hardy."

"I am, too." Emily held her baby a little tighter.

"You have a lot to learn about safeguarding a child's welfare."

Emily would get no argument there.

"Uh, Em…" Stepping from the shadows, Jonas looked uneasily between his sister-in-law and Kit. "Sean called. Kit's supposed to pick up Alex."

Without another word, Emily turned and disappeared into the house.

Jonas, awkward and uncomfortable, stepped out on the front stoop. "Alex is around the side." He waited for Kit to descend before following her.

"You know," he offered, "Emily's not so bad when you get to know her."

"If you say so."

"Sure, she can be overprotective at times, but— and I'm not telling anything that isn't public knowledge—Emily was adopted. As much as the Chestertons love her, I think she wonders why she was given up in the first place. As a result, she clings more tightly to her own children, to her family. She's a good wife and mother. A loyal sister."

"You don't owe me an explanation."

"I feel I do." He scratched his head. "You two seem to have some bad mojo going. If you're going to hang with Sean and Alex, you need to see Emily's good side. She needs to see yours."

"Rumor in town has it I don't have a good side."

"Not according to Sean." Jonas shook his head.

"And I've never known my brother to be a bad judge of character." Frowning, he shifted on the balls of his feet, as if he'd intervened far more than he was used to doing.

"Thanks," Kit said. It couldn't have been easy for Sean's brother to have offered as much as he had.

"Kit! You're here!" Alex raced around the corner of the house, her cousin Noah at her heels. "Where's Dad?"

"He got tied up at the pier. Says he'll make it another day. So it's just the two of us."

Alex covered any disappointment quickly. "If Dad's not coming, can Noah?"

"I only brought two kayaks."

Alex's hopes sank. She sure wanted to show off Kit and those kayaks to her cousin. He'd been going on and on about the new baby.

And if Dad's whistling before he went off to work this morning—after his date last night—meant anything, her dad had a new girlfriend. And maybe that meant Alex would get a new mom. And…that could mean she might possibly, someday have a new baby brother of her own. At the very least, they might get a dog.

You gotta have dreams, Dad always said.

"Sorry, Noah." She shrugged, not altogether unhappy that she'd have Kit to herself for a few hours. "Catch ya next time."

Noah scowled. "I wanna go."

"Me, too, buddy," Uncle Jonas said, "but it's girls' afternoon out." Alex could always count on Uncle Jonas to try to make things right between the cousins.

"Okay." Kit looked at them as if she cared how they might feel. "I have six kayaks. One day—if your mom agrees, Noah—I'll let you and your dad, and your grandfather and your uncles borrow them for a boys' afternoon out. What do you say?"

"Yes!" Uncle Jonas answered so fast he startled Kit, but Noah still pouted. What a baby!

"Come on, Kit!" Disgusted with her ungrateful cousin, Alex grabbed her friend's hand.

"See you later." Kit looked relieved.

The two of them ran across the lawn and the street and down the embankment to the little beach. Alex was so happy she felt as if she could fly.

"So," Kit said as she held out a life preserver. "Is your cousin okay with being left behind?"

"Sure." Alex hopped into the shiny red kayak, leaving the blue for Kit, then hoisted the lightweight, double-ended paddle. She felt like an explorer already. "He'll get over it."

But as she and Kit paddled down the harbor toward the islands, and as Uncle Jonas got in his truck and drove away, Alex looked back to see Noah run across the road. She watched as he untied the old inflatable rowboat from the army-and-navy surplus store. The kids were allowed to play in it—with a buddy—as long as it stayed tied up by a long rope to the post on the beach. If Aunt Emily found out he was taking it out in the harbor just to prove he was cool, he'd be in big trouble. Such big trouble Alex bet her aunt wouldn't let Noah go for boys' afternoon out. And that would be his tough luck. Sometimes her cousin couldn't see the forest for the trees, as Pop Pop often said.

Alex shrugged as she turned to catch up with Kit. Noah wasn't her problem this afternoon. She wanted to find out if Kit had as much fun on that date last night as Dad did.

"Hey, Kit! Wait up!"

Kit quickly turned her kayak—these things sure could maneuver—and came up after Alex. They played tag among the lobster boats and the yachts at their moorings and the flocks of mallard ducks, and Alex thought how much fun it would be to have a mom as cool as Kit. It would be so easy to call her Mom, but if she wanted to be called Kit, that was okay, too. The name didn't matter.

"Race you to that island!" Kit called, pointing to Little Bit, the island right across from the pier. It was so small you could get around it in fifteen minutes—not so great for exploring—but there wasn't much poison ivy and you could watch the lobstermen working the pier. Maybe they'd even see Dad today—and there was a great old skeleton of a rum runner's boat that had run aground in a storm back when Pop Pop's pop was a kid. Kit would really like that. Alex would let her use her Swiss Army knife to carve her initials right alongside Alex's and Dad's so that a little bit of Kit would always be right here in Pritchard's Neck.

Her kayak glided up on the shore beside Kit's. "These are awesome!" Alex couldn't stop grinning. "You gonna keep 'em here?"

"In Pritchard's Neck?" Kit looked kinda shy. "I was thinking about it."

"I know you're gonna let the boys take 'em out—" Alex seized the moment "—but you're gonna take Dad out, aren't you? Just you and him."

"Now why would I do that?" Hopping out of her kayak, Kit smiled.

"Because if you liked the first date, you're supposed to go on a second one." Alex rolled her eyes as she got out of her kayak. Kit was smart, but she was being real slow here. "You did like the first date, didn't you?"

"Did your dad?"

"Oh, yeah!" Alex was surprised Kit couldn't tell.

"Me, too." Kit avoided looking at Alex. "Let's get a couple big rocks to tie the lines to."

"Don't have to. The kayaks are pulled up high enough. The tide's going out."

"Are you sure?" Kit looked at her the way her teacher did when she didn't believe some geography fact Alex had told her.

"I've lived here my whole life." Alex stuck her fists on her hips. "I should know tides."

"Okay!" Kit threw up her hands in surrender. "I believe you know tides."

Alex just loved Kit for believing in her.

Feeling almost giddy, Kit followed Alex around the tiny island. What a terrific day! Blue skies. Plenty of sunshine. A soft salt breeze. An enthusiastic companion. And...a lover waiting back on shore. A woman could get used to this.

"No!" Alex's voice broke into her reverie. "Carve your initials over here. Near Dad's and mine."

How did she come to have a Swiss Army knife in her hand? How much time had she spent with her head in the clouds? She needed to pay attention to the here and now. She was looking after an eight-year-old. An adventurous eight-year-old.

She looked at the spot on the faded wooden hull where Alex wanted her to carve her initials. This child was doing everything in her considerable power to involve Kit in her world.

Despite a little voice that warned her not to become ensnared, Kit carved *K.D.* right next to *S.M.*

and *A.M.* When she was finished, Alex took the knife and carved a big heart around the three sets of initials. Kit could barely keep back tears.

"There," Alex declared. "Now let's check out if we can see Dad at the pier."

They rounded the last outcropping of rock along the shore, and saw, not Sean at the pier, but two kayaks—their kayaks—drifting a long cold swim away from the island.

"Oops!" Alex squeaked, covering her mouth.

"Oops?"

"I guess the tide was coming in, not going out."

Oh, my God, she'd trusted an eight-year-old as if the child had been an adult. Kit groaned. What a lack of judgment on her part. She was definitely not parenting material.

"Help!"

Before Kit could shuck her T-shirt, shorts and sneakers and go in after the kayaks, she turned to the sound of a child's voice and saw Noah, not much closer than the kayaks, but in the opposite direction. In an inflatable boat that appeared to be sinking.

"He doesn't have a life preserver!" Alex cried. "Kit, do something!"

Even if she could throw that far, their life preservers were in the kayaks.

Without a second thought, Kit shed her clothes

down to her bra and panties, then plunged into the Atlantic waters. She was a strong swimmer, but the cold took her breath away. Dear God, she prayed, keep that boat afloat until I can reach the child.

At that moment Noah's flimsy boat suddenly slipped beneath the surface of the water, leaving the boy clinging to a plastic oar that would, all too soon, betray him as well.

"Help!" Noah's voice was weaker now. The water must be all of fifty degrees, if that. Shock could set in before too long.

With forceful strokes, Kit cut through the water, concentrating on the small wet head bobbing maybe seven or eight yards away.

As she came within grasping distance of Noah, he slipped beneath the surface of the water.

She dove.

Through the clear, frigid water she saw his small form drooping like a jellyfish. She grasped him, surprised by his body's lack of substance, and kicked for the surface.

When they broke, she sucked in air. Cupping her hand under his chin and resting his head on her shoulder, face-up and well above the surface of the water, she stroked with her free hand as if pursued by sharks. Noah didn't resist. She wished he would. Wished he'd flail around. Show signs of life. But he remained a small, still lump floating beside her as she willed her cramping muscles to perform, to get them both safely back to shore.

She calmed her rising alarm by focusing on what she must do. What she would do. She would get this boy ashore. She would administer CPR. She would wrap him in her dry clothing. She would shout so that the men at the pier could hear her. Could come for Noah. Despite the burning in her chest, despite the creeping numbness in her fingers and toes, she stroked.

She could hear a desperate keening from shore. Alex. And men's voices from the pier. Shouting. And motors. They'd noticed. But it was up to her—right now—to get Noah to safety.

When her feet touched bottom, she propelled herself out of the water, carrying Noah to a tussock of marsh grass. She lay him on his back. Cleared his mouth. Tilted his chin. Placed her mouth over his and breathed. She counted out the length of the breaths, counted out the intervals between. Interspersed the mouth-to-mouth with careful but deliberate pumping, her crossed hands on his tiny chest.

She ignored Alex's wails. Alex would survive this trauma. Noah needed her now.

As she was about to place her mouth over his again, his head lolled to one side and he vomited. She gently rolled him on his side as a flotilla of motorized dinghies ground ashore. Led by Sean, several lobstermen clambered over the rocks and grass.

Someone wrapped her in a scratchy blanket that smelled strongly of dog. Someone else wrapped Noah in another blanket.

"He's conscious!" came a relieved cry as the sound of an ambulance siren wailed down Pier Road. In the confusion, Alex threw herself at Sean.

"I'll ride with him," Sean declared as one of the men loaded Noah into a boat. "Karl, take Alex to my dad at the pound. Bert, see that Kit gets to Frederica Harpswell's. Make sure Frederica gets a doctor to look at her."

"I don't need—"

"Don't argue, Kit," Sean commanded, boarding the boat with Noah. "I can't stay with you and with Noah."

"Of course not."

As the small motorboat sped away toward the pier with Sean and the lobsterman with Noah, and another whisked Alex away, the man named Bert picked up Kit's T-shirt, shorts and shoes. "Let's get you where it's warm. I'll round up your kayaks later."

She didn't care about the kayaks. And doubted she would ever be warm again. She was out of her league when it came to the overwhelming responsibility of children. She'd been given a chance and she'd blown it.

"I'm s-s-sorry," she stammered, shivering violently. "I'm…so…sorry."

"Don't be," Bert replied with a gruff kindness. "If it wasn't for you, that kid coulda been in a heap of trouble."

How had this happened? Could she have prevented it? Was Kit in so much of a hurry to get away from Emily's house—so concerned with her own needs—that she didn't recognize the steps to take to protect the child? Didn't fully comprehend the temptation two new and colorful kayaks posed?

And Alex…this was the second fright she'd had with Kit. The child was tough, but surely she would bear some emotional scars. There was no doubt Kit had come into the McCabes' lives and had wreaked havoc.

Dammit, Sean was a fool to have trusted her.

Letting Bert guide her to the remaining boat, she knew what she needed to do.

"AT THE FIRST SIGN of difficulty, you're going to turn tail and run?" Teacup in hand, Frederica stood above Kit, eyes flashing. "I'm afraid I expected more mettle of you, Kit."

"My mind's made up." Kit took the offered tea, then pressed herself farther into her chair by the fire, pulling the goose-down duvet more closely around her. "I'm leaving tomorrow."

"I don't understand you." Frederica looked drawn, and for the first time, old. "Heroically, you saved a child from drowning, yet you haven't the courage to let a man and his daughter love you."

She didn't. The idea of family and children terrified her. She was no good at it. And not being attuned to family and children wasn't like not being good at bartering in a bazaar or mending your clothes with a bone needle or pretending you were unfazed by drinking snake's blood. Not being good at family and children brought dire consequences.

She heard the doorbell ring.

"It gets easier," Frederica insisted. "Parenting. Especially in pairs."

Kit didn't believe her.

Karen appeared in the doorway with Sean right behind her.

"Are you okay?" he asked, crossing the room to her chair.

"Is Noah?"

"Absolutely." He smiled. "Thanks to you."

"No." Putting her hand up as if to ward off a blow, she untangled herself from the duvet. Pushing out of the chair, she stood before the fireplace with her back to Sean.

"I'll leave you two," Frederica said with discretion.

Kit wanted to scream at her to stay. She wasn't strong enough to be left alone with Sean.

"What's wrong?" As Frederica's footsteps faded, he stood behind her, tried to draw her back against his chest.

She stepped away. "I'm leaving. Tomorrow."

"And you'll be back…when?"

She turned to face him. "I won't."

"Don't do this to me, Kit." His face held no surprise, only anguish. "To us."

"There can't be any us. I'm no good at us." She wrung her hands. "I'm a loner, Sean. Always have been, always will be. When I attempted us this week, I made an unholy disaster of it."

"What are you talking about? You saved a little boy's life today."

"That little boy wouldn't have been out on the water in that unsafe raft if he hadn't been following the kayaks. If he hadn't been following Alex and me. He wouldn't have been there to see the police haul Stu and me off in patrol cars if he hadn't been following Alex. Who was following me."

Feeling as if a dam had burst, she couldn't stop the flow of words. "I'm not the kind of role model Alex needs. She needs more structure, not less. Someone who can help her fit in. If it were just a case of you and me…but it's not. You're a package deal, Sean. You. Alex. Her cousins. Your family. Everyone you love deserves someone they can count on—"

"Stop it." He moved to take her in his arms, wouldn't let her slip away. Pulled her hard up against him. Lay his cheek on the top of her head and held her tight. He almost made her feel safe.

"You're beating yourself up over stuff that happens," he argued. "It just happens. Not only to you, but to families. Ordinary, chaotic, frustrating families like mine." He stroked her back. "The McCabes are capable of generating our own messes, thank you. My dad claims he's never seen the end of a Super Bowl. They all got interrupted with trips to the emergency room with one or another overactive kid who needed stitches or a bone set. You're no better or no worse an influence than the rest of us."

"I can't—"

"Yes, you can." He took her by the shoulders and held her so that she was forced to look him in the eyes. "And if you want to talk it out, I will…but not tonight. I came by to tell you the kids were okay and to check on you. But Alex's principal has thrown us a curve. She wants to do Alex's evaluation first thing tomorrow instead of Friday. Says the last day of school is too crazy. I have to get back to Alex, who's understandably clingy at the moment. I have to get together all her schoolwork from the last week and a half. I have to plan out what I want to say to convince Candace Simmons it wouldn't be right to retain a bright and curious kid just because her social skills need work—"

"She wouldn't!" Kit flinched at the outrageous possibility.

"She might." Sean caressed her cheek. "So you see I'm not putting you off. You've got to rest. I've got to think of Alex."

"Of course."

"But we will talk. Tomorrow. As soon as I get things squared away at school."

He pulled her into a kiss that prevented her from answering. From making a promise she wouldn't keep. He was wrong in thinking she could fit into his life. What about Babe? He didn't even know the secret about Emily. No, there were many reasons Kit couldn't stay with him. But that didn't prevent her from fitting herself against his body, from accepting his kiss, from making him hers for a few more seconds.

When he released her, he frowned. Her distress seemed to have rubbed off on him.

"What's wrong?" she asked.

"I'm sorry." He rubbed a hand over his forehead. "I'm not giving you the attention you deserve tonight. I need to make you understand. You need to know that I'm the one who's responsible. Ultimately."

"For what?"

"Alex." He let his hands drop to his sides. "And what kind of a father am I if I can't stay focused long enough to keep one small eight-year-old on track and out of trouble?"

Kit read his subtext. She was the distraction.

CHAPTER SIXTEEN

KIT HAD TAKEN the coward's way out by leaving Frederica a goodbye note. It would be better not to leave a note for Sean. A clean, sharp break. More painful, perhaps. But a keener inducement to forget her and move on.

The thought nearly broke her heart.

Her knapsack packed and stowed in the Harley, Kit cruised through Pritchard's Neck one last time, glad for the wind in her face. A perfect excuse for the tears in her eyes. She was leaving the place that had both denied her a real home and then had held out the tantalizing prospect of one.

Approaching the elementary school, she thought about Sean and Alex's evaluation meeting. Would the powers that be really hold a child back when her only "problem" was that she didn't fit a pre-conceived mold?

Kit saw Sean's truck parked next to the message board out front that read Have a Great Vacation! Character Words for the Summer—Friendship and

Loyalty. Hell, Alex could teach the course on friendship and loyalty.

Kit pulled into the parking lot. She couldn't leave town without making a last stand for the first person to wholeheartedly champion her.

Inside the building, her boot heels clicking on the linoleum floors, the never-changing odors of a typical school making her uneasy, Kit saw the glassed-in meeting room next to the principal's office. Saw, too, the entire McCabe clan assembled, seated in chairs and facing a panel of school personnel. She should have known Alex wouldn't need her help.

She paused, about to turn around and leave, when she saw Alex, small and miserable, scrunched in a chair next to Sean.

She pushed open the door.

"I'm sorry, but this is a private meeting," Candace said. "My secretary next door—"

"It's this meeting I'm interested in. I have something I'd like to say."

"I'm afraid this evaluation is restricted to faculty and family."

"Let her speak." Sean rose from his seat. His voice held an authority to match the principal's. The warning look he tossed at his family clearly said he'd brook no objections. "Kit knows Alex as well as anyone here."

He gestured to his chair for Kit to sit, but she remained standing by the door.

She stared at the so-called education experts on the panel arrayed behind a long table at the front of the room. It felt like a courtroom, the proceedings like a trial. The heavy-handedness of the whole affair angered her.

"You haven't devised a test that can measure Alex's intelligence, creativity and heart," she declared, staring into the faces of each of the panel members in turn.

"You'd have to spend a day with her on her father's lobster boat. Observing her understanding of the lobster trade, a trade that involves biology and math and mechanical science and weather and oceanography, to name only a few disciplines. You'd need to go to tea with her at Frederica Harpswell's to see her passion for reading and writing and geography and world history."

As Candace's eyes opened in surprise, Kit swallowed hard and forged on. "School is supposed to prepare you for real life. Alex has already embraced real life with gusto. And as for those character words on the sign out front, she could teach the lot of you the true meaning of loyalty and friendship. And tolerance. And acceptance."

Hitting her stride, she rolled on. "This eight-year-old sees beyond the surface. Beyond stereotypes and rumor. She rejects 'perfection' to find the good in people."

Kit approached the staff table. "Yes, Alex's a little different. But would any of you like to be judged on your differences? A weight problem, a speech impediment, an impending divorce, financial difficulties." She noticed some of the members of the panel squirm. "Isn't it more productive when people foster your strengths and potential?"

Sean grinned. Alex sat up in her seat. The other McCabes leaned forward as one.

"You are educators," Kit chided, her fingertips on the table's edge, leaning forward. "You should be looking for ways to bottle Alex's insatiable curiosity and open-mindedness. You should be building a system that respects each child's unique personality and learning style. That would be education."

Moving quickly, Kit gave Alex a tight hug, then left the conference room, knowing Sean couldn't follow. He would stay to defend his daughter before the panel.

But Kit didn't count on Emily slipping out of the meeting. She called out just as Kit stepped out the front door.

Pretending she didn't hear, Kit walked toward her Harley.

"Kit! Stop! Please!"

The *please* held an unexpected note of humanity and stopped Kit in her tracks. She turned slowly to face her sister.

"You were right all along." Figuring she'd cop to her guilt and shorten Emily's tirade, Kit raised her hands. "I'm not responsible enough to look after children. I'm not a good role model. If I stayed, I'd just screw up Sean's and Alex's lives. That's why I'm leaving town." She reached for her helmet.

"I...I want to...thank you for saving my son." Emily's words were halting, but the tone was sincere.

Speechless, Kit stared in disbelief into a pair of pale gray eyes that matched her own.

"Perhaps I wasn't responsible yesterday," Emily went on. Carefully. "Perhaps I wasn't as vigilant with Noah as I should have been. But that doesn't mean I shouldn't go on being a parent. Trying to be the best I can be."

Kit couldn't get past the woman's unexpected thank-you.

Frowning, Emily cleared her throat. "Alex has been as happy as I've ever seen her this past week. Sean, too. Perhaps...I was...wrong to begrudge them their happiness."

"Perhaps." Kit put on her helmet. "But it's a moot issue now. I'm leaving."

"Noooo!" Rocketing out of the front doorway, Alex threw herself at Kit. "You can't leave. I love you!"

"I love you, too," Kit replied as she wrapped her arms around her small body.

Alex buried her face in Kit's neck. "I want you to be my mom!"

"Oh, honey!" Controlling her tears, Kit unwound Alex's embrace, then held her at arm's length where she could look into her eyes. "I have no experience as a mother. I would be terrible."

"That doesn't matter." Alex looked at Kit with such earnestness. "I've had lots of experience being a daughter."

"Alex." Sean suddenly loomed over them. "Go back inside with Aunt Em," he said gently. "I need to talk to Kit."

"You sure do." Alex hugged his waist before putting her hand in Emily's. "Don't blow it, Dad."

Sean took a deep breath. He had no intention of blowing this last chance with Kit. This was the woman he wanted to spend the rest of his life with. If he hadn't completely known it two nights ago after dinner and lovemaking, he sure knew it now after her courageous and impassioned speech in Alex's defense.

This woman was an original. He was not letting her go this time.

"You were going to leave without goodbye," he said when Alex and Emily had returned inside the building. "Why?"

"For a lot of reasons."

"I have time."

"What about the meeting?"

"It's over. The panel will call me back in when they've made their decision." He removed her helmet. "And, by the way, you were terrific in there."

"I only told it as I saw it." She fiddled nervously with a toggle on the Harley's storage compartment. "To try and make up for some of the mess I've caused."

"Mess? You've caused? Fill me in, Kit, because if the last week has been a mess, I want more of it."

"You want your family giving you grief for a relationship with me?"

"My family's all but come around. Emily is genuinely thankful to you for saving Noah." He reached for Kit's hand, which she didn't pull away. A good sign. "Sure, things may always be prickly with Emily. She has her own queen bee way of doing things. That's just Emily."

"What about my mother? Her reputation? My reputation?"

"You can't deny your mother. Or be held accountable for her behavior. You've done nothing but try to make things right in the wake of her irresponsibility." He smiled. "I think your heroics on Little Bit erased any lingering doubts in town about your character."

"But Stu Hardy—"

"I think a lot of people had their eyes opened where Hardy is concerned. I'll be looking for a new handball partner. Do you play?"

"I could learn. If I stayed." She shook her head as if she didn't quite believe she was having this conversation. "But if I stay, can I still speak my mind, or do I have to undergo some small-town cutesification? Do I have to smile and suffer fools silently?"

"I'd like to see the person who'd try to make you." Chuckling, he turned her face up to look into those ever-changing gray eyes. "There will always be fools. But we'll try to keep them out of your line of vision. Frederica. Alex. And me." He kissed her lightly on the lips. "We want you to be happy."

"But—"

"No buts. I love you, Kit. Stay with me and Alex."

Tears forming in her eyes, she glanced away from him. Down the road. He read her mind. It would be so much easier—for her—if she left town. Now.

He wasn't going to let her take the easy road.

"Running will solve nothing," he said with all the conviction he could muster. "Not when both Alex and I love you. Need you."

She placed her hands lightly on his chest as if

to keep him away. "I have so little experience in real love. Just look at how I rejected my mother three days ago. My own flesh and blood."

"You didn't reject your mother. You exercised tough love." He placed his hands on her shoulders. "All love is tough, Kit. The road is sometimes rocky, sometimes smooth. Joy and fulfillment."

She looked up at him as if she wanted to believe him.

"You brought the joy back into my life," he insisted. "Stay. Marry me."

"Marry you!" Surprise and longing filled her eyes. "But you live here, and my work takes me around the world."

"You don't think I haven't stayed awake nights worrying about that one?" He ran his hands up and down her arms. "And I think I have a plan. One hell of a plan, if I do say so myself."

"A plan?" Could it be interest—real interest—crooking the corners of that luscious mouth, dimpling those silky soft cheeks? "What's your plan, Mr. McCabe?"

"Okay…" He felt an adrenaline rush at the boldness of his proposal. "In season, I lobster and run the pound with my father and brother. You run kayak tours. Here in Pritchard's Neck. Alex can bounce between us and day camp. She'll think she's died and gone to heaven."

"And in the off-season?"

"Ah, here's the genius of the plan." He couldn't help the big grin that spread across his face. "In the off-season we all travel with Seafaring Cecil."

"Haven't you forgotten about Alex and school?"

"I'm thinking Alex needs a shot at alternative schooling for a while. Home schooling."

"Home schooling?" Behind her incredulity lay an eagerness. "How would that work?"

"You can get guidelines and standards off the Internet. We'd have to submit lesson plans and stay in touch with the school system here in Pritchard's Neck. But how we meet the standards is up for creative interpretation."

"In a classroom that could encompass the world!" Her face lit up.

"Absolutely!" He knew she'd understand. Knew she couldn't help being intrigued. "We'd have our cake and eat it, too. Home and travel."

"You'd be willing to do that?" Kit couldn't believe Sean had thought this through so thoroughly.

"Be willing to do a job I love in a town I love and travel the world with the woman I love? Why wouldn't I be willing?"

"Alex would love it." Who was she trying to fool? She would love it.

"And you wouldn't hate the idea of spending part of the year in town?"

"Sean…I think my traveling has been a search for home. As long as I'm with you, I'm home."

"I guess my restlessness was all about craving…something. The something missing in my life." He brushed her cheek with his fingertips. "You've filled that empty spot. Quieted the restlessness. Travel with you and Alex would be different, a shared experience."

Tears fill Kit's eyes. She'd been afraid to let herself dream of a future with Sean, had been overwhelmed by their differences. How could she say no to such a man?

"Do you love me?" he asked, his eyes full of love for her.

"I think I always have."

"Will you marry me? Be my wife? Alex's mom?"

Her response was to kiss him deeply, passionately, publicly. It was a yes understandable in any language in any country around the world.

Alex pushed through the front door of the school to see her dad and Kit kissing. Ms. Simmons had asked Alex to get her father so that they could talk about whether Alex was going on to fourth grade or not. It had seemed like such a big deal until right now. Until Alex saw the kissing. Ms. Simmons could wait.

Dad and Kit turned and saw Alex in the doorway. Kit had tears in her eyes. Happy, not sad tears. Dad was grinning to beat the band. "Shall we tell her?" he asked Kit.

"You'd better!" Alex sang out as she dashed to be included in their hug. "Tell me what?"

"How would you like to be in a wedding?" Kit asked, wiping her hand across her eyes. "Your dad's and my wedding."

"Do I hafta wear a dress?"

Kit laughed. "You can wear your lobstering boots for all I care!"

"Then count me in!"

Dad swung her up on his shoulder, then wrapped his free arm around Kit. Together, like a real family, they headed for the school to tell the rest of the family the cool news.

Happily, Alex thought about the trick to getting a mom. Picking just the right person, then being very patient until that person and your dad realized what was best for them.

Piece of wedding cake.

EPILOGUE

Late Summer

KIT STOOD in Frederica's solarium, staring at the McCabe family assembled in chairs on the back lawn. Was she really and truly about to marry Sean? Join this family? If her hands weren't holding the magnificent bouquet from Frederica's gardens, she'd pinch herself. Good thing. It wouldn't do for the bride to walk down the aisle all black and blue.

Chessie poked her head into the room. "Are you almost ready to take the plunge? The natives are getting restless."

"I will be as soon as my attendant shows up. Any clue where she might be?"

"I think Frederica's helping her with some finishing touches."

Kit grinned. "With Alex, that could mean anything!"

"Oh, I think the two of them are turning that little dog into a ring bearer. This will be a wedding to remember." Chessie enveloped Kit in a hug. "You look beautiful, sis." Not sister-in-law, but sister. From the beginning Chessie had welcomed her with open arms.

Kit was going to have to learn a whole new vocabulary word: acceptance.

"I'll see if I can hurry them along," Chessie suggested. "If I can't, I'm afraid Sean may carry you away and elope."

"Hmm. Not a bad idea."

"Very bad idea." Chessie shook her head. "The crowd will not be denied its entertainment."

As Chessie left, Millicent Crenshaw bustled through the room with a tray of champagne flutes. "Never fear! Everything's under control!" she sang out, crossing the room toward the tent outside, followed by several wait staff in crisp black and white. It had been Frederica who'd suggested using Millicent's catering services for the reception. Kit had balked, especially since Ed had slunk back into town expecting his wife to take him back, only to have her hand him his possessions already boxed. But when Kit had finally approached Millicent, the caterer had gladly agreed, adding, "We survivors need to stick together." Millicent also agreed to provide the box lunches next summer for Kit's kayaking day trips.

Kit smiled and looked back out the window where she caught a glimpse of Emily surrounded by her husband and children. Since the rescue of Noah she'd been civil, and civil was good enough for Kit, who'd come to a decision about the secret. Family was what you made it. Emily was a Mc-Cabe, née Chesterton. She would never be a Darling. If she ever wanted to make contact with her birth mother, that was between Emily and the Chestertons. If they needed help in the search, well, Kit was always there. In the meantime, Kit had her own family to forge. And maybe—some-day—another child. Who knew? That was the beauty of this family-as-a-state-of-mind theory.

"Ta-dah!"

Kit turned to see Frederica in an enormous picture hat and gauzy dress, and Alex in a miniature safari outfit, complete with pith helmet and riding crop. "Where did you find that?" Kit exclaimed, delighted.

"In the same place you found your wedding dress!" Alex said. "Frederica's attic!" Kit was wearing Frederica's own wedding dress, an exquisite satin sheath embroidered with thousands of handblown beads.

"And what have you done to Bitsy?" Kit knelt beside the papillon who wore a velvet pouch around her neck.

"She's the ring bearer!"

"And I thought Chessie was kidding." Kit hugged Alex. "You look like a true adventurer."

"Just like you!"

Frederica opened her arms to Kit. "You, my dear, are about to embark on the most fantastic adventure of your life."

"Thank you." Kit wrapped her arms around Frederica and inhaled the floral scent of the woman who had become like a mother to her. "For everything."

"Thank you, love. You have enriched my life."

"Let's get this show on the road!" On tiptoe, Alex peercd out the window at the guests. "Everybody's here."

"Then places, everyone," Frederica declared as she ushered Alex out onto the patio, to the long white carpet that rolled its way down to the sea and the waiting clergyman. Jonas stepped up, gave Frederica his arm, then walked her to the front row of chairs where she would wait to give Kit away.

Babe had not been invited. She hadn't even been told of the wedding. The hurt was still too fresh. Kit's survival instincts, and a new overwhelming protective instinct toward Alex, too strong. She'd made one concession. She'd spoken with Babe and had agreed to let her mother use her Boston apartment until the lease ran out at the end of the month. Babe had found a job and had also discovered that there were far more men in the city than in Pritchard's Neck. She'd forgotten about coming back.

With joy in her heart, Kit moved to step onto the patio.

"You are so beautiful." Sean's quiet voice surprised her.

She turned. "What are you doing here?"

"I'm on my way to the altar, but I couldn't wait to see you." He looked so handsome in his navy suit. Tanned and rugged. And hers.

"Isn't this bad luck?" she asked, sure that it could never be. Not with Sean.

He stepped forward to take her hands. "We seem to be making up the rules as we go along."

"Does that make you nervous?"

"No. It makes me feel free."

"Me, too." She squeezed his big, work-roughened hands. "Now get out there. I want to marry you."

"And I want to be married to you. Forever."

He kissed her lightly on the lips, then stepped onto the patio where he also kissed his waiting daughter.

Kit gave him two minutes to take his place at the far end of the white carpet before she walked through the doorway into the best of all adventures.

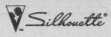

SPECIAL EDITION™

THE ROSE COTTAGE SISTERS

Love and laughter surprise them at their childhood haven.

What's Cooking?

SHERRYL WOODS

**Silhouette Special Edition #1675
On sale April 2005!**

Fleeing a burgeoning romance with a renowned playboy, food editor Maggie D'Angelo escapes to Rose Cottage, vowing to put love on the back burner. But Rick Flannery intends to turn up the heat, and soon Maggie is face-to-face with the sexy fashion photographer who makes her blood sizzle!

**Meet more Rose Cottage
Sisters later this year!**

**THE LAWS OF ATTRACTION—
Available May 2005**

**FOR THE LOVE OF PETE—
Available June 2005**

Only from Silhouette Books!

HARLEQUIN®

AMERICAN *Romance*®

THE ABBOTTS

A Dynasty in the Making

A series by

Muriel Jensen

The Abbotts of Losthampton, Long Island, first settled in New York back in the days of the *Mayflower*.

Now they're a power family, owning one of the largest business conglomerates in the country.

But…appearances can be deceiving.

HIS FAMILY
May 2005

Campbell Abbott should have been thrilled when his little sister, abducted at the age of fourteen months, returns to the Abbott family home. Instead, he finds her…annoying. After a DNA test proves she isn't his long-lost sister, he suddenly realizes where his prickly attitude toward her comes from—and admits he'll do anything to ensure she stays in his family now.

Read about the Abbotts:

HIS BABY (May 2004)
HIS WIFE (August 2004)
HIS FAMILY (May 2005)
HIS WEDDING (September 2005)

Available wherever Harlequin books are sold.

If you enjoyed what you just read,
then we've got an offer you can't resist!

Take 2 bestselling
love stories FREE!
Plus get a FREE surprise gift!

Clip this page and mail it to Harlequin Reader Service®

IN U.S.A.
3010 Walden Ave.
P.O. Box 1867
Buffalo, N.Y. 14240-1867

IN CANADA
P.O. Box 609
Fort Erie, Ontario
L2A 5X3

YES! Please send me 2 free Harlequin Superromance® novels and my free surprise gift. After receiving them, if I don't wish to receive anymore, I can return the shipping statement marked cancel. If I don't cancel, I will receive 6 brand-new novels every month, before they're available in stores. In the U.S.A., bill me at the bargain price of $4.69 plus 25¢ shipping and handling per book and applicable sales tax, if any*. In Canada, bill me at the bargain price of $5.24 plus 25¢ shipping and handling per book and applicable taxes**. That's the complete price, and a savings of at least 10% off the cover prices—what a great deal! I understand that accepting the 2 free books and gift places me under no obligation ever to buy any books. I can always return a shipment and cancel at any time. Even if I never buy another book from Harlequin, the 2 free books and gift are mine to keep forever.

135 HDN DZ7W
336 HDN DZ7X

Name	(PLEASE PRINT)	
Address	Apt.#	
City	State/Prov.	Zip/Postal Code

Not valid to current Harlequin Superromance® subscribers.

Want to try two free books from another series?
Call 1-800-873-8635 or visit www.morefreebooks.com.

* Terms and prices subject to change without notice. Sales tax applicable in N.Y.
** Canadian residents will be charged applicable provincial taxes and GST.
All orders subject to approval. Offer limited to one per household.
® are registered trademarks owned and used by the trademark owner and or its licensee.

SUP04R   ©2004 Harlequin Enterprises Limited

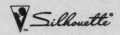

SPECIAL EDITION™

presents the next three books
in the continuity

MONTANA MAVERICKS

GOLD RUSH GROOMS
Lucky in love—and striking it rich—
beneath the big skies of Montana!

THEIR UNEXPECTED FAMILY
by **Judy Duarte**
SE #1676, on sale April 2005

CABIN FEVER
by **Karen Rose Smith**
SE #1682, on sale May 2005

And the exciting conclusion

MILLION-DOLLAR MAKEOVER
by **Cheryl St.John**
SE #1688, on sale June 2005

**Don't miss these thrilling stories—
only from Silhouette Books.**

Available at your favorite retail outlet.

YOU, ME & THE KIDS

On sale May 2005

High Mountain Home
by **Sherry Lewis**
(SR #1275)

Bad news brings Gabe King home to Libby, Montana, where he meets his brother's wife for the first time. Siddah is doing her best to raise Bobby, but it's clear that his nephew needs some male attention. Can Gabe step into his brother's shoes—without stepping into his brother's life?

On sale June 2005

A Family for Daniel
by **Anna DeStefano**
(SR #1280)

Josh White is trying to care for his late sister's son, but Daniel's hurting so much nothing seems to reach him. The only person the boy responds to is Amy Loar, Josh's childhood friend. Amy has her own problems, but she does her best to help. Then Daniel's father shows up and threatens to sue for custody, and the two old friends have to figure out how to make a family for Daniel.

Available wherever Harlequin books are sold.